CW00971263

Water & Glass

Water & Glass

Abi Curtis

First published in the United Kingdom in 2017
by Cloud Lodge Books (CLB)

A CIP catalogue record for this book is available from the British Library.

ISBN 978-0-9954657-5-6

1 3 5 7 9 10 8 6 4 2

Print and Production Managed by
Jellyfish Solutions Ltd
Cloud Lodge Books Ltd (CLB)
51 Holland Street, London W8 7JB
cloudlodgebooks.com

for Gabriel

Almost forgetting for the moment all thoughts of Moby Dick, we now gazed at the most wondrous phenomenon which the secret seas have hitherto revealed to mankind . . . No perceptible face or front did it have; no conceivable token of either sensation or instinct; but undulated there on the billows, an unearthly, formless, chance-like apparition of life.

Herman Melville, Moby-Dick, 1851

The *Baleen*

Nerissa watches the monitor. A wraith hangs there in the grey-green static, mournful face closed, giving up no secrets. She examines the feet, noting their development. The heartbeat blips steadily, turned down low. This life is just beginning. Nerissa doesn't know how it will fare here, aboard the *Baleen,* below decks in the dark blue light. Reva shuffles as the transducer rolls over the rough, grey skin of her abdomen. Her legs move like classical columns, slowly shifting against the wooden boards.

"Shh," Nerissa soothes, running a hand down Reva's trunk. Reva plants her wet mouth against her arm. Up to seven months to go. Reva has been carrying this baby for fifteen months already, twelve months before they boarded the *Baleen*. So patient. Nerissa wonders if she knows instinctively what is forming inside her. She eyes the sonogram a little longer, the short trunk, the ghostly, hollow eyes. She tries not to dwell on the day when Reva will finally give birth, hoping it will not be here, on the wooden deck, the other creatures curious and afraid around her, listening to her deep moans. They had only managed to bring two elephants with them, both female, one African, one Asian. The African died a month ago. Nerissa could not determine the cause, partly because she did not have all of the equipment she needed for an autopsy. She wondered if the elephant knew she shouldn't be here, below the ocean, if she recognised the plains of her homeland were submerged and felt herself to be drowning. They had been forced to heave the silver body into the ocean. She thinks of it resting on the seabed now, like a beautiful fallen oak. The largest creature aboard the *Baleen* now gone. Perhaps one day they could do something with the DNA sample Nerissa keeps safely labelled in the freezer. Perhaps not. Such science no longer exists, and many backward steps have already been taken. She pats Reva, who gives a low rumble and settles back into her pen.

Nerissa hoists herself up the creaking steps, and back into her workroom. The place is something between a veterinary surgery and a makeshift laboratory, entered through a low, oval door. The floors are rough wooden boards, hastily pushed together and varnished. Along one wall is a white, polished countertop with two steel sinks set into it and Formica cupboards underneath. A steel table is in the centre, with leather straps for restraining larger animals, or keeping them steady if the waves are rough. Nerissa has a variety of monitors, some salvaged from hospitals, others from an old consulting room. There are two computers, one for admin work, another larger one for displaying X-rays, sonograms, cardiographs. She's grateful for the taps that filter the seawater, and the hot tap that works intermittently. Nerissa connects her portable transducer to the large screen, watches the images load. She notes each measurement, thinking about what to name the calf. 'Shem' for a boy, and 'Ruth' for a girl?

Nerissa works mostly alone, her clients, the animals, themselves shifting on the deck beneath. Her past life is only a few months behind her, but it feels like a decade ago. It seems an age since the bungles and triumphs of her training: poring over textbooks with images of organs and veins, blue and red and labelled in an unfamiliar language. She remembers the first animal she worked on, with its tiny beating heart, how it died in a quiver on the table, and the first that came back to life, stitched up and wagging. She gained experience whilst she studied, by volunteering at a clinic not far from the college. She cycled to work each day with the sea breeze salting her face, never knowing quite what the hours might bring: a deer snagged on a fence, panicky and beautiful; a parakeet, stubbornly flapping in the corner of the consulting room; a thin, knowing stray, submitting to her touch. She had never been able to get used to putting an animal down, to the owner burying their hands and face into its furry neck and weeping their goodbye. But she had loved bringing the rag-tag queue passing through the surgery back to health, back to being with their owners, who more often than not loved them as they would love a child.

She found herself drawn more and more to stranger animals: sly salamanders, rolled-up hedgehogs, leverets with their long, alien limbs. Whilst many of her clients thought of their pets as human, she fell in love with creatures for their difference from humans. The way an owl sees the edges of the world, and lives for the darkness, or the way a dog can smell the invisible guilt on a person. The opportunities came for exploration and volunteering. Her work took her to Asia, where she encountered canny orangutans in the forests of Borneo. Then she met Greg and learned to dive. Greg with his clever eyes, with his way of touching her lightly on the back of the neck to ease her fears before she dived in. It was Greg who introduced her to the humpback whales. They were ancient, like slow-moving cities from past centuries. She had to overcome her phobia of water to dive with them, her legs trembling in the grey-blue shadows. One passed close by, a dark eye swivelling; she felt the pull of the current as it went. She saw barnacles freckling its skin. She felt great joy in its total dismissal of her, as if, for a moment, she were without body or soul and did not have to fear again. That was before her time at the Institute, and before the floods had truly come. Before she had made her choice.

"Dr Crane." Herman slips in, an empty feedbag over his shoulder.

"All right, Herm." Nerissa smiles at the way he still calls her 'doctor', a title that, as she's explained, does not match her qualifications.

"I'm worried about the Komodo dragon. He's a bit aggressive. And he looks all raggedy."

"I'll have a look later. Don't worry; he might be shedding." She sighs. "And getting used to it around here. They don't live so long in captivity, but they do become quite tame."

Herman notices the images of the elephant foetus. "Whoa, look at that!" His bristly red eyebrows lift, his dry, full mouth pushing out. "Like a miniature ghost-elephant. Is it doing okay?"

"Seems to be doing well."

"A mister or a miss?"

"I can't tell. It was being shy and I couldn't get the angle."

Herman looks pleased, as though the dry straw and feed he's given Reva has formed this new life. The animals still fascinate and frighten him. A caretaker for a school in his past life, he is short, auburn-haired, with powerful arms and all the bulk in his torso. He's happier here than ever before, breathing in the musk and damp of the lower deck, learning the looks and sounds of the animals, mucking out their enclosures, checking his list for their many different meals. At fifty-five he feels the buzz of an apprentice, and his years of loneliness are stinging less and less. When he thinks of what his lot might have been, he thanks that lucky ticket. He links his hands and cracks his knuckles, like thunder before a storm. Nerissa winces.

"I wish you wouldn't."

He grins, showing crooked, but spotless teeth. "Want some of that yucky powdered tea?"

"Sure, two sugars. By the way, any sign of that Woolly Rat?"

Herman looks grave and stands close, as if someone might be listening. He comes up to her shoulder, smelling of cinnamon and wet straw, a hint of dung.

"Molloy? He's AWOL, Doctor. I don't get it. He liked me, even liked to be touched. Do you think we should make it known?"

She sighs, resting her hips against the cold examination table.

"No, it will only cause panic. He likes people, we know that much. But we don't know too much else about them. I expect he's after a mate, and is a bit more of an escape artist than we thought."

"Aren't we all?" Herman winks, jovial again, pattering out of the room. Nerissa can't be sure which part he's referring to.

Molloy is a favourite of Herman's and Nerissa's. They have only one Woolly Rat aboard. They were never able to save a female, so had planned to keep a sample of his blood frozen, when they had the chance. He was one of a handful of new species found in remote rainforests in the early twenty-first century. She can't remember the dates, but had read about them in her training textbooks. She watched the recording, grainy with age, of the team that found his ancestor. She heard the catch of excitement in the zoologist's voice as he explained they had no fear of humans, as they'd never encountered them before. He had held the specimen by the tail.

Molloy stood out from the other animals, partly because of his affable nature, partly because of the small device he had attached to his head. It was like a tiny crown, giving him the air of a scruffy and shambolic monarch.

"It's a camera," she had said at his first assessment. He'd snuffled at her palms, and a low purr had come from his throat as she stroked his sides.

"I think he must have been part of a survey. It's still recording. And maybe transmitting." She looked at the tiny orange light inside the plastic casing.

"Amazing. What I'd give to see what's on this." She thought of the lush rainforest. A rat's-eye view. Huge, turquoise butterflies; multi-legged insects trooping the floor; tiny emerald frogs ricocheting from leaves in a downpour.

"Can we?" asked Herman.

"I've no idea how. It's probably transmitting to somewhere. But I know nothing about this stuff."

"Is there a frequency? Is that what you mean?"

"I guess so."

She had thought of her own face, peering into the tiny eye of the camera. Molloy had looked back up at her and licked her elbow like a dog. They had decided against removing the camera. It was attached expertly, and they didn't have anything they could remove it with safely. And they didn't want to destroy the footage; perhaps they would find a way to watch it at some point. She treats him differently to the other creatures, letting him sit by her as she reads through her textbooks or charts about the different diets of the animals. Sometimes, if she is sure Herman is not watching, she talks to him, telling him her favourite stories of the life before. A part of her likes the idea her private murmurings are being recorded to be witnessed long after she is gone. She likes to run her hands along his thick, warm fur; it calms her as she reads, or thinks about the day's tasks, and in return, he purrs and grinds his yellow teeth. She should not be attached to him, but she is; he reminds her of her first fascination with creatures not like herself.

She's not sure why Molloy should have suddenly taken off, but in a way, she envies his escape. After three months aboard, it feels like there is nowhere to go. She misses his odd companionship, his quivering face and shining eyes, the hot little belly that touches the ground when he scuttles along. She misses feeding him morsels of her own food as she reads through her notes, his yellow teeth and quick mouth crunching them down.

She is still getting used to this strange life—Herman for company, the face of Captain Holmes appearing on screens around the *Baleen,* to give a speech or explain their position. She wonders when she'll meet him. There has been no sign of land for months now, and no indication there will ever be. The *Baleen,* named for its whale-like shape, can totally submerge if necessary, but at present the lower decks are below the water and the upper decks above. It is part submarine, part ship. The decks below water are dusky with rippling shadows, long and with curved walls, subterranean-like huge caves. On these decks, it is like being Jonah lost in the belly of the whale. A whale the size of a village. The decks above the waterline are bright with the sun; its off-white light is spread by fog and cloud, casting long shadows over the wood. There are several viewing stations where the portholes are wide and tall and you can watch the sea. Nerissa goes every day. On Deck Five she looks out at the silvery, curved horizon and sees nothing but endless water. And on Deck Eleven, just above the animals, she watches the ocean, and sees even less: a soupy, uncannily empty blue. A terrifying blue that shouldn't be. The sea haunts her.

In the mornings, for the first few seconds after she wakes, she never remembers where she is. And when she does realise, she thinks of how they are never in the same place twice, but pushing through the dark blue sea as if moving deep into the heart of a shadow. Sometimes she sleeps poorly, thinking of Greg, her arms tingling for him as if she might touch him. At other times, she sleeps as if dead; dreamless, heavy sleeping that leaves her with pins and needles in her back.

Sometimes Nerissa dreams. It is always the same dream now. It is too dark to see. There is only a faint orange glow visible in the distance. She hears dripping. She puts out her hand, feeling a pillar to her right. It is hard, damp, and slimy. The air is thick with the smell of minerals, metallic and earthy. She hears a voice. It is a man's voice, far off, echoing, so she cannot tell if it comes from in front of her, or behind, from the left or the right. As her eyes adjust, she sees another huge pillar, then another. She steps forwards, walking between the pillars, touching their damp, chilled surfaces as she goes. Each pillar she reaches reveals another in front of it, as if she walks through a forest of stone. And still the voice is calling, insistent, not seeming to come any closer, but not growing farther away.

Then a new sound, from ahead: a rushing that becomes a roar. A roar that grows and overpowers any other sound. Something white ahead of her is advancing, rising. She realises too late it is a wall of water, roaring through the pillars, coming for her. It washes over her head. She cannot hang on to the pillar she hugs; the water rips her away and drags her back. All noises cease except for a muffled sound. She is underwater, and there is no air above now. She opens her eyes to see huge golden carp and glittering coins beneath her. She breathes in and out, mimicking the 'O' shapes of the carps' mouths. She does not drown. The water is like thick, heavy air. She fans her fingertips and regards them in the bronze light. Then she wakes.

It is always this dream, and though no harm comes to her, she wakes in a sweat with the sheets twisted around her and her breath fast, as if she has come up for air. Why doesn't she wake up when the water roars towards her? Isn't that what most dreamers would do?

Each morning, there is that same queasy feeling as she goes to the mirror and dampens her face, the same heaviness in her abdomen. But there is also a hollow feeling there. She knows what this is: the weird feeling of guilt she carries. It aches like a bruise. She peers at her face in the strip-light. Her skin is dry and flaky, her lips cracking. She licks them; they taste metallic. She rubs neat petroleum jelly into them, then into the scaly skin at her elbows. She feels tired down here, headachy and raw, an edge of seasickness always lodged in her throat.

When she was with Greg she felt beautiful under his hands, under his gaze, and because he told her so. Now she avoids mirrors except for when she wakes, seeing the dusky brown of her skin, increasingly dry and flaky no matter how she tries to soothe it; her winter-coloured eyes; her thick, coarse dark hair. Just before the flood, she had it cropped like an urchin. Greg called it her mid-life crisis, though she's barely into her thirties. He also said it was sexy and smoothed his fingers into it. "Hello, beautiful neck; you've really been hiding." It has grown out now and sticks up at the sides. She doesn't like to venture onto the service decks, and has only gone far enough to find food, occasionally something she can adapt into an implement for work. But soon she ought to find a hairdresser and get her straggly mop seen to. She's tall and lean, but dresses in ill-fitting clothes, whatever she has, breathing in to do up the waistbands.

She pulls off her calico apron, the closest she can get to the white coat that used to make her feel professional, and rests back into a cracked leather armchair, another mismatched accessory in her surgery. This is where she'll re-read the few books she managed to save, or look over her charts and notes. She'll wait as long as possible before she goes to her quarters for the night. She lives on the same deck as the surgery, one deck above the animals, so that she can be close in case of emergencies in the night. Like every single person's room, it has a tiny cubicle shower; a bed that folds from the wall; a kitchen unit and a porthole (at the moment submerged) facing the empty underbelly of the ocean. Nerissa hangs a length of cloth over it.

Sometimes she'll walk along Deck Five as the vendors close their trade for the night, watching the lights go out before she descends by ladder or lift to her bed. Tonight is different; tonight, she does not have to avoid the blank sea. She can instead be on the lookout for Molloy.

Deck Five

Nerissa takes the capsule lift to Deck Five. It judders on its pulleys, and she grips the hand-loop that hangs from its transparent roof. Deck Five is where the vendors serve their food, or offer their wares—a collection of makeshift, mismatched tables and stands. Some of the stands are becoming more substantial, turning into booths, as vendors find more material to add to them. Some just use a sheet of metal or plastic resting across two empty barrels; others, with more aesthetic sensibilities, have sawn and fashioned wood, melted and moulded plastic into seats, or found old chairs for customers to sit on. There's no money on the *Baleen*, and supplies are limited, so everyone on board is allocated tokens at the beginning of each week. Brown tokens are for food. Nerissa, along with Herman and some younger helpers, takes care of a clutch of animals that provide eggs and milk, as well as tanks of freshwater shrimp, small molluscs, and some saltwater fish. She is hoping that someone is trying to catch fish from the sea, but she is not allowed above Deck Three to find out, and has still seen no signs of life through the portholes. This thought troubles her. Otherwise, most food is vegetarian, grown on the Garden Deck, Deck Three, where the sunlight streams in. The oxygen from the garden is stored for emergencies. Nerissa has only experienced the *Baleen* fully submerged once, just after she came aboard, when the first wave hit, rolling over the top of the ship with its full violence, perhaps for an hour, maybe two. She had wrapped herself up in blankets in her new quarters and wept, that terrible guilt washing through her body, establishing itself in her bones.

She hands a token over to a vendor who is shutting up shop a little later than the others. The man is tall, with a wide waist, a carefully trimmed brown moustache, and blue, almond-shaped eyes. He has shredded some red and white plastic bags above his stall to create a decorative awning. He has a flat, tarnished plate onto which he spreads a pale, thin batter. It crackles and solidifies, forming a crêpe.

"Lemon and sugar for you? Or a little cheese? I could spare a couple of sea-snails, since it is the last few orders of the day." His accent is deep and sticky. He might be Belgian. The sweet smell of the batter makes Nerissa realise how hungry she is, with a little stab of nausea. The vendor looks her up and down.

"You know, you could be entitled to a few more tokens, if you ask the stewards."

"I don't need them, thanks. Can I have cheese and one or two snails, if you can spare them?"

He is pleased with this, grinning and pushing out his chest. Most passengers have not got used to the slimy, chewy texture.

"Great protein, no?"

"Mm."

Nerissa rests against a barrel and folds pieces of the crêpe into her mouth, taking the quick, full bites she has formed the habit of. The flesh of the snails bursts wetly on her palate. The vendor watches her, cleaning his implements, collecting tokens into a plastic box. Other vendors are doing the same or have already left their stalls bare and empty until tomorrow. A steward quietly patrols, glancing at them as she pauses to turn back up the deck.

Stewards wear green smocks, always with a utility belt of some kind around the waist. It might be made from an old jeans belt, a gardening apron, even just a length of rope with hooks sewn into it. All carry a radio, which they occasionally murmur into, and all carry something else that looks like a barcode scanner, or a large brush. Nerissa imagines, since they have no weapons, that it's some sort of stunner, or Taser, or pepper spray.

Nerissa knows of no violence on the *Baleen* so far. All of its occupants know it is a great privilege to be saved, so she has never seen this piece of equipment in use. There was certainly violence in the time before; the kind that comes from fear and a need to survive. But not here, in this aftertime, which seems like an end and a beginning. Or a beginning and an end. As time goes on there could be violence. People will begin to feel confined—she has seen this in animals before and knows she will again, and humans aren't too different in this respect. People may develop aversions to certain personalities—not everyone can get along. It depends on how long they have to be here, waiting, pushing slowly through the sea.

Nerissa and the vendor smile at the steward. She has a rosy, gentle face that reminds Nerissa of her Aunt Elaine. The vendor smiles back and continues walking away along the deck.

"You want some water?" asks the vendor.

"Water?"

"To drink."

"Oh, yes. Yes, please."

She sips. The water here has a hint of salt and chlorine. But it is good; it revives her and her thinking clears. The vendor is wiping the table.

"You don't come here during the day; why not?"

"I don't know. I'm shy about the crowds, I guess."

"It's nice up here. Like a market. People talk, they laugh. People are beginning to make friends. It's good to see."

She smiles, leans her head onto her arm.

"What is your name?"

"Nerissa Crane."

"A beautiful name. I'm Gus Duras."

He clasps her hand, his fingers thick and hot.

"What do you do?"

"Ship's vet."

"Ah, very important."

She smiles, swallowing down the last of the crêpe.

"I even look after these snails I'm eating."

"Well, what a betrayal."

Gus chuckles, deep from his belly.

"Come up here more often. Talk to people. There are people from all over the world here. You will make friends." He looks down for a moment, avoiding her gaze.

Gus steps out from behind his stand, pulling a sheet of metal over his hot plate, securing it with a padlock.

"It is late, Ship's Vet. You know they don't like us out on the decks past dark. Why don't you go to Social?"

Something in her resists the idea of the ship's new community, its rituals and attempts to make people bond. She prefers the close cocoon of her memories.

"I'm a bit of a night owl. I like this place when it's quiet."

"You do? I find it creepy myself."

The dusk is settling, the sky beyond the portholes deepening to Prussian blue. Green and white lights give the now deserted deck a low illumination, as if the *Baleen* were completely submerged, even here, where the deck is just above the water line.

"I must go home to my wife. Good evening to you, Nerissa Crane."

Gus wanders along the deck to the lift, pausing a moment to view the purplish sliver the sun has left behind. Nerissa wonders what Gus's story is. He has his wife on board with him, which pleases her somehow, though she realises she knows nothing about either of them, or what they may have left behind. Perhaps she will try to come here more during the day, to dive into the bustle and noise of the deck when it becomes an international market. Fruit, vegetables, and even flowers from Deck Three; books read and wanted for swapping; mended clothes; old musical instruments; the scrap stall that she sometimes scours for old electricals, or cutlery that can be sharpened and adapted for surgery.

Large pipes run between decks for ventilation, water, waste, for the engineers to check the *Baleen's* secret workings. Perhaps

Molloy has found his way into one of these in-between spaces, drawn to the snug darkness, reminded of his earthy home in New Guinea. Perhaps he's attracted by the voices echoing from the decks; the friendly shouts of the vendors, families arguing in their quarters before bed; mothers singing to their babies to soothe them before sleep, the sounds merging into pipes or cavities, quivering in his whiskers. The Bosavi Woolly Rat, one of the last new species discovered, with no fear of humans, the size of a spaniel, with his small, clever eyes, and his fluffy cartoon face.

Nerissa pads along the length of the deck, the wood creaking and giving as she goes. She peers into the dark limit of the walkway, unfinished and raw, like the edge of a makeshift stage. She looks around. There could be cameras surveilling her. She wouldn't be surprised. She eyes the blank screen suspended above the deck, four-sided like the information centres in a port. Captain Holmes appears on these screens and talks to them. He has a handsome, debonair look, the slight droop to one eyelid only enhancing his charm, his hair swept neatly under his peaked hat. His messages are generally upbeat, often practical. When they boarded four months ago, messages were frequent, sometimes twice daily, telling them where to get tokens for food, dos and don'ts, health and safety. Everyone stopped to listen, turning to the screens in reverent, anticipatory silence. Nothing ever seemed unreasonable. The captain and the crew working beside him. They saved them. But sometimes these screens now seem as if they might also be watching. Now they are black and dark, reflecting only the still, empty deck.

In the dim, green light, Nerissa wanders to the bow-end of the deck, where part of the inner wall is unfinished, and there is a jagged gap. The boards that make up this deck also end abruptly here, their raw edges partially concealed by the curved inner wall. Nerissa peers into the gap. There is a slight drop, of six feet or so, and she looks down at the uneven metal pipework on the surface below. She turns her head, left and right, at this gap between walls, suddenly aware of the layers that separate her from the pressure of the sea. There is writing here, graffiti of some kind. No Molloy, blinking in the shadows, but this text. She smiles. The teenagers are rebelling, expressing themselves. She's already stir-crazy; she can't imagine what they must feel. They would love the raw, hidden, off-limits darkness of the ship and want to put their mark on its blankness. She sits, and then lowers herself down into the space below, her feet balancing on the pipes. Moving a few inches, she realises this little nook can't be seen at all from up on deck. If you slipped in unnoticed, you could hide here all day. The graffiti is painted on the inner metal skin of the *Baleen*. It reads:

STOWAWAY LIVES ON

The idea of a stowaway on a ship like this is strange, but not unthinkable. She frowns, rubbing her fingers over the coloured letters. They are thickly written and deliberate, defiant as a shout in a silent room. She hears and feels the low hum of the *Baleen* pressing on.

A beam of light is suddenly in her face. Behind the light, up on deck, is a dark silhouette.

"What are you doing down there? Did you fall?"

"No. Sorry." Nerissa squints into the torchlight, shielding her eyes. She makes out the shape of a steward. A hand reaches down and the torch recedes. It is the steward with the face of Aunt Elaine, kindly, with a certain annoyed crinkle at the corners of her eyes.

"I was … I was a bit lost."

Nerissa takes her hand, allows herself to be pulled up.

"We don't like you to be out late." Still kind, a gentleness in her Irish voice. "Just in case you fall. Why don't you go to Social, or back to your quarters? How did you end up down there? Is there something … ?"

The steward scans her torch into the corner.

"No, I just dropped my watch. It's a man's watch, bit loose on me, but here, I found it."

Nerissa holds up her slim wrist, Greg's watch slipping down. The steward frowns, blowing a tuft of hair from her eyes. She is wearing deep pink lipstick and a touch of rouge. Nerissa thinks of make-up counters in department stores, how long it has been since she has seen one of those.

"Well, perhaps you need to punch another hole in the strap. See the Mender tomorrow. What do you do on board, my love?"

"I'm the vet."

"Ah, so we must be careful with you."

"I'll go to bed. I'm sorry. I still have trouble sleeping." Nerissa doesn't know why she has admitted this. Maybe because she would admit such things to Aunt Elaine.

"Of course. It's the sea," the steward says softly. "It's always been this way, back to when fishermen told their tales, kept their superstitions. Some people are just troubled by the sea; they know it has a rogue heart. But you learn to love it." She pauses a moment, then smiles. "You know, if you can't sleep, there is a party tonight, in Social. Why don't you go along?"

Nerissa smiles, feeling a strange fluttering sensation in her abdomen in response to the steward's words. She still can't bear a crowd of people, the liveliness of a party. It will only make her think of Greg, how she longs to see his terrible dancing, and his laughing face.

"I'm too tired," she says, "but thanks." She heads back into the lift, juddering down to Deck Eleven and her bed.

Starlings

The last time Nerissa saw graffiti would have been at Port Mandelbrot—the day she boarded the *Baleen*—something aggressive daubed under a bridge or on the side of a disused building. Someone angry because help was promised and didn't come in the end. She flops onto her back on the narrow bed, pulling off her plimsolls with her heels. Greg is never far from her thoughts, and he comes back now.

They were in Old Brighton, on a weekend trip, the streets still damp and silty from a recent flood. She wore Wellingtons over her jeans, and her feet were an inch underwater. It was a good weekend for browsing the streets, the shopkeepers optimistic again, the sun bright, giving a green tint to the few ragged clouds. They had lived here once for a year, while Greg was on an assignment. He would head down to the ruin of the Palace Pier most days, at sunset or dawn, photographing the thousands of starlings that flew in formation at the rising and setting of the sun. The sight was astounding: a dark cloud undulating, lifting, falling, reshaping like a rapid weather system.

One sunset, they went together, and the starlings were there in their great murmuration. Nerissa felt the vibration in the air, caught glimpses of their quick, clever faces. Greg got closer and closer, leaning out over the edge of the barbed wire to get a better shot. Then he had turned to her, his eyes shining.

"Riss, I'm going to go onto the pier. I can get right in the centre of them, then. The pictures will be amazing."

"No, Greg, it's not safe," she had pleaded, looking around her at the desolate, empty beach and the heaped grey clouds. But she knew he would ignore her. At times like this, it was as if he were possessed, his face to the camera, his body leaning towards his subject. The energy of the starlings dragged him in.

Climbing under the barbed wire and nailed planks had been easy enough. Most people didn't need to be deterred, and no one had checked them for years. Some people even knew what had happened to the West Pier, long before they were born. They'd seen images of the raging, orange fire and a much earlier generation of starlings hovering, homeless, like a thundercloud merging with the thick, black smoke. The planks were rotten and flaking, the barbed wire rusting in the briny air. She had watched him walk gingerly across the crumbling decking and saw the structure sway with only his weight. Greg had stood inside the murmuration of starlings, at its eye, when they choreographed their farewells for the night, the sun slipping down like a copper penny in a slot. The photos captured the details of their wings beating in unison, the roll and turn of their huge storm. Locals said there were more now than there had ever been when the pier was open. Greg heard the birds like the sound of heavy rain, felt the air shifting against his face.

The waves troubled the structure, and the wind had got up. She heard the pier creaking; tears rose in her throat. The starlings lowered their great shadow down. Greg walked away from her, slowly, to the end of the shifting pier, down to where the old rides still stood, hollowed out and drained of colour. She watched him go and held her breath until he had come back towards her. Then he disappeared into one of the old booths; a painted hand indicated this was where the fortune teller used to work. As he did, Nerissa heard a crack. One of the boards of the pier began to lift, weakened by his step, pulling out the wood where Greg stepped. He leapt away as it crashed into the grey waves below and spiralled down into the water.

"Greg!"

"I'm okay." His voice was muffled by the wind. He edged precariously around the hole in the floor, out of the booth, reaching for her hand; grabbing for anything to hoist himself back over. The structure groaned again, as if he had set something off and the whole thing might fold away into the sea. Nerissa had not been able to reach him. She put one foot on the rotten wood, and he stretched for her hand. Another board went at his left foot, crumbling down, and he made a grab for the barbed wire, which bit into his skin. A droplet of blood ran down his arm. Then he turned and pushed himself over the barrier. His face was flushed. He was smiling. He hugged Nerissa to him.

"Damn, that was a bit close."

She had looked up at him, pushed her hands into his chest, and slapped him hard across the cheek. He was silent as she walked away, her hair flying in the wind, but a smile played on his lips as he brought his hand up to his smarting face.

Greg had brought home his beautiful, desolate images. These were some of the photos of which he was most proud. The helter-skelter still striped like a humbug, spiralling down. The ghost train, more haunted than it had ever been when in use. The skeletal tracks of the roller coaster, rising into a sky heaped with clouds, silvery light leaking through. The carousel was the bleakest image to Nerissa: those bright, gypsy horses, grey in the black-and-white photo, their eyes blank, as if lonely and anticipating riders, their names printed under their elaborate saddles. Florence, Lightning, Rosy, Shadow.

He spoke of them on that later weekend visit.

"Remember those shots, Riss, of the birds?"

"The starlings. Yeah, stunning. But it was dangerous, you know, what you did."

"I know." He sighed. "I'll never hear the end of that."

It was always this way with Greg. He wanted to be in the heart of things. He wanted to push it. She was fearful of danger—collapsing structures, unpredictable waves. Now she wonders if her feeling of wanting to draw him close, keep them both safe, was the wrong one, if his lovely risk-taking, which had excited her so much at first, was right. No one was really safe; she knew now that was all illusion. The sea outside the *Baleen* is silent, but full of rage. She doesn't know what happened to those pictures. She had them framed and displayed them in their apartment when they were at the Institute. But now she can only see them faintly. Sometimes even Greg's face is hard to recall.

She thinks about the pier now whilst she stares at the watery light, faint on the ceiling of her quarters. It must have collapsed by now, the bodies of those carousel horses resting underwater in mid-canter, looking up to the clouds beyond the surface. And where are those starlings now? Have they found another structure in which they might roost, or are they rolling across the sky in a great, pulsing ball of wings, searching for dry land? Nerissa tries to concentrate on the good memory of that weekend visit: wandering with Greg's arm around her through the narrow, winding lanes. Looking at antique jewellery in the windows, eating burgers from a stall. They went to see some beautiful graffiti in the back streets, commissioned and approved by the council. A trompe l'oeil chess set with funky pieces, a narrative poem in elegant script over a painting of a scroll. The artists who had studios under the arches on the seafront had been flooded out, waterlogged over the years as the shoreline crept ever closer. Commissions like these helped them survive.

Greg adored this place, its slightly rebellious nature, its openness towards difference. That was a precious day, and somehow, they knew it at the time, although they didn't understand why. They were kind to one another. He bought her a stack of postcards from the flea market, and some Deco glasses that looked silly on her. She bought him the strong coffee that he loved, though she knew it made him over-talkative and tiring, and a battered tweed jacket that he wanted, with a fusty smell. It was the last time they visited Old Brighton. Months later, after the rain stopped and the flooding dried, after the city was thriving again, one of the first waves came over it, rushing through the cobbled and colourful streets, up to and then beyond all but the highest blocks. After, only the top floors of the high-rises remained. The sea spread out, reaching parts of the Sussex Downs, still and bright under a blue sky. Beautiful, if anyone had been left to admire the view.

Nerissa sleeps now, finally exhausted by her thoughts, that coloured writing on Deck Five floating into her dreams.

The Mender

When Nerissa wakes, she goes to her porthole and peels back the cloth hanging there. The water is dark, but this time, instead of the usual emptiness, there is something floating. She leans forwards and presses her nose against the cool glass. It is some sort of worm, transparent, so that the thin cord of its being is visible like the mechanism of a spring. It glimmers, pulses, and darts away in seconds. The floods of the last three decades have caused ocean life to retreat down into the farthest depths, whilst a soupy layer of algae and pollution sits on top. This is the first time since coming aboard the *Baleen* that she has seen anything living in the sea. She tells Herman at breakfast. He's been to Deck Five for fresh bread, and also has a pot of marmalade.

"I think that baker has a thing for you," says Nerissa, leaning across the steel table in her surgery, scattering crumbs. Herman blushes, a high colour creeping up his neck and into his ruddy cheeks.

"I don't think so. She's too young for me."

"So why always the free jam?"

He shrugs, wiping his knife over the warm bread.

"Tell me more about this thing you saw, a worm, was it?"

"Something like that. I only saw it for a second—can't be certain."

"But you did see something? Couldn't have been a trick of the light? Something in your eye left from sleeping?"

"Definitely saw it. You sound like you don't believe me."

"No, course I do." Herman stands, slapping the crumbs from his front. "I'm pleased—it's a good sign."

"I thought so."

There is a silence. Herman goes to wash his hands at the steel sink. He looks over at Nerissa, who is staring at the metal table, touching the leather straps. She sometimes zones out like this. He knows she must be thinking about her old life. He does it too, occasionally. But he was already doing it before the *Baleen*. He doesn't feel the need to dwell on things here. His other life has been relatively easy to let go of. He thinks of Frances, the baker, her floured hands wrapping his breakfast into paper.

"Bring the paper back tomorrow, Herman; it doesn't grow on trees, you know." Frances chuckled as she told him this. He hopes it's because she wants to see him again, but perhaps she says this to everyone. Soon, he'll head down to the animals, to their grunts and squeaks in the indigo light. He washes his hands once more. Nerissa is looking at him.

"Herm, I'm going to wander around the ship a bit today. I'll check the animals with you in the afternoon."

"Where are you wandering to?"

"Just the market. I don't go up there enough; I need to get to know a few people."

"Yes, good plan."

There's an expression on Herman's face that Nerissa can't quite grasp. It could be sadness, or pity.

"Just beep me if you want me for anything," she says.

"S'all right. I'm beginning the lessons today. One of the stewards asked that I take some kids to show them how we take care of the animals, what we feed them, that kind of thing."

"That's great." Nerissa is pleased. Though she helps Herman with the animals in Deck Twelve, he won't let her do the heavier work. He's old-fashioned in that way. He sees her as the brains, himself as the brawn. Nerissa can only imagine the chaos of coordinating this: taking animals from the flooding and derelict zoos in all the cities they could get to. She likes the idea that younger passengers learn what happens here, the importance of the creatures. She tries not to think about all the species left behind. She worries about the cramped conditions those saved must live in. She hopes it will not be long.

She remembers going to one of the last legal zoos as a small girl, a place where they aimed to conserve animals. A panther paced inside her enclosure. She was midnight black and glossy as an oil slick, turning her hips back and forth. She stared at Nerissa with amber eyes, dropped her velvet jaw, and offered a deep rumble. Nerissa watched her through the thick glass for a long time, believing they were communicating in some way. Her mother grew impatient and left her there after a while. Nerissa only looked away when the panther slipped into a pool of water surrounded by rushes, and was gone like a shadow.

There are no panthers on the *Baleen*. The lioness they have is semi-tame, having been bred in captivity. She has two cubs and is fairly placid for now. Nerissa does not know if the land they find will be suitable. The stewards don't seem worried. They acquired the lioness and housed her on the ship; they must have plans for her. Nerissa needs to know more about these. Her unease about the future of the animals is building. Herman has gone down to Deck Twelve. She wipes the crumbs from the table and takes the lift to Deck Five.

Nerissa speaks to the steward with the face of Aunt Elaine. This time, on the sun-flooded deck, she can see her name badge: *Tabitha*. Tabitha is friendly, helpful as a woman in a shop. Nerissa is reminded of department stores again. The noise and bustle of Deck Five surrounds them. The vegetable stall to their side smells earthy and bright.

"It's just that there haven't been any messages for quite a while now, about our destination. About how long things might take. We can feed the animals, but I'm concerned about space, about their welfare."

"We don't know much at the moment. It's early days. We're on a course for land. We hope to improve living conditions, and we're already expanding some decks. It's best to see most things as temporary."

Tabitha is repeating herself, reworking, in that soft Irish lilt, what she's already told Nerissa. Her answers are fair enough, but Nerissa is impatient. She has always been this way. She thinks that the stewards, at this level at least, do not know much.

"Can I speak to the captain? I just need a few more specifics. Or does the captain have a deputy or something?"

"Yes. I will relay a message for you. I will ask the captain if you can see him, or his first officer."

"And what's the first officer called?"

The steward pauses for a moment, shifting her belt around, looking for something in one of its pouches. She produces a notebook.

"The first officer is Darshana Hardy."

She notes something in her book.

"What's your name?"

"Nerissa Crane."

"And you are the ship's vet?"

"Yes. And I want to know our destination, and approximately how long we will be at sea."

"You know the danger we were in, don't you, Ms Crane?"

The comment is furtive, spoken under the breath. Nerissa is not sure she has heard, or interpreted, right.

"Of course," she says. "I almost didn't make it on. I saw … I saw a lot of things."

She looks down, pushes the toe of her plimsoll into the gap in the decking. She looks back up, into Tabitha's eyes, which shift away from her, then return.

"I only need to know a bit more detail, so I can plan for the animals. I'm prepared for bad news—that land is months away, or everything will take a long time to rebuild. That's okay."

The steward is suddenly more like Aunt Elaine again. She smiles.

"Of course. I'm sure the captain would like to meet you; you are a doing a valuable job. Your quarters are in Deck Eleven? I would just ask one thing: that you don't say too much to others. News travels fast on a small vessel, and some are afraid of the animals. Ideas get distorted. Already, some have asked about your deck, wanting to know if there is anything dangerous kept down there. If anything could escape." She looks to the decking at her feet. "And there have been complaints of noises. We tell them this is normal. The dark of the sea, its own sounds and movements, can spark the imagination, so it can."

Tabitha seems to be curious herself, as to what stalks Deck Twelve, but she doesn't ask directly, so Nerissa chooses not to say anything about it.

"I won't talk about the animals with anyone—not my concerns about them, anyway."

The steward smiles, satisfied, puts the notebook back into her belt, and heads away along the deck. She disappears into the crowds around the vendors.

It is mid-morning, a busy time. Some passengers are grabbing a quick bite, others are stocking up for the evening. Nerissa sits on an upturned crate while the Mender, a leathery old man, punches an extra hole into Greg's watch. Her watch. He does it quickly, and then lifts it to the light, his cracked, thick-skinned fingers gently holding the face. He looks at Nerissa, his green eyes bright against mahogany skin.

His voice is soft, with a hint of the Central European about it. "This is a good piece. As good as any I've seen. Kinetic. Waterproof to a decent depth. Where did you get it?"

"It's my husband's. He used it for diving, sometimes."

"Tell him he made a good choice."

"It was a gift from me."

"Ah." The Mender nods, arranging his bradawl with the other tools. He has a series of battered metal pots; an expandable toolbox powdered with rust; a hot iron; some steel thread. Nerissa thinks he can probably fix most things, but not everything. He seems to be ignoring her now as she straps the watch back on, as if she's already walked away. The watch fits snugly, but its face still looks big and out of place on her wrist.

"Watch-making was what I did," the Mender says, perhaps to no one, still looking down at his tools, wiping and rearranging them. "There wasn't too much call for it in recent years. And I couldn't begin again here, not with this equipment."

Nerissa nods. She regards him for a moment.

"Can I ask you something?" she says. "Do you have any idea where we're headed? I can't tell, and no one has told me."

He looks at her. She feels as though she's already broken her promise to the steward, and that somehow, he knows.

"I'm the vet. I look after the animals on Deck Twelve. I'm hoping they won't be cooped up too long." Her heart quickens, and that falling sensation in her abdomen is back.

The Mender smiles kindly and replies, "I've guessed we may be travelling south-east, towards the Indian Ocean, then up towards Asia, just judging by the position of the sun. Perhaps we're heading even farther. It's approximate; I'm no expert. I think that's our best chance of unflooded land. How your animals will fare, who knows."

"So, how long will it take?"

He shrugs.

"Seems to me we're travelling slowly now. Probably to conserve energy. It could take weeks, maybe months. If you speak to the captain, he'll know."

"Have you ever spoken to him? He seems pretty elusive."

"Is he? Have you asked to speak with him? He meets people when they ask."

Nerissa feels bad now, trivial even. She thinks of the responsibility Captain Holmes and the crew have taken on. Of how frantic they must have been, how busy and uncertain they must be now. How they are shielding the passengers from fear. She has no reason to think he won't see her. She has considered herself too important in the scheme of things. She feels herself flush with shame. The Mender appears not to notice.

"We'll get there," he says.

Nerissa smiles, gives a small salute, slips off of the crate, and walks back into the market.

Molloy

hears sounds above him, regular low thumps, and soft creaks. The pads of his paws touch the damp, and his claws slip on something smooth. There's an echo above that rolls around the walls of the pipe, a scent of plant through a crack, then the tang of meat. The camera catches a swinging view of the metal pipe, light seeping through tiny holes, a puddle of damp on the ground. He longs for worms. He's only found small beetles, which he crunches until they ooze against his tongue. His whiskers quiver, measuring the space, gauging whether he can squeeze his plump body through, his fur flattened and slick. A voice he knows comes to him from far away. A voice he doesn't know joins with it. He tries to follow, swivelling his papery ears to where he thinks it is emanating from. But then the sound bounces, shatters into the walls of the pipe, dissolves. He pauses, watching the shadows, then moves on, creeping, testing the ground. He is close to something. Blue-green light suddenly filters from above, strings of it rippling. He decides to climb towards it, certain of someone up there.

Crêpes

Nerissa passes a stall of bric-a-brac, things salvaged, brought aboard, and not wanted. People are crowding around, picking over old china cups; cameras that may be waterlogged; silverware; tangled, glinting jewellery. The vendor here is a young woman with dreadlocked strawberry-blonde hair. She barely looks up, keeping her eyes on the jumble, shifting and turning the items as people put them back down. People still worry about theft, but it is rare. Nerissa eyes an old butter knife, but she has something similar and sharper in her surgery.

She makes her way to Gus Duras's *Crêperie*. There are two customers before her, waiting. Gus recognises her, offering a grin as he deftly spreads the batter onto the crackling plate. As he curves the batter round and flips, she notices how quick he is; it's almost too quick to see it happen. The hairs on his arms scorch and shrivel in the hot steam, but he doesn't flinch. He has someone with him today, a tall, lanky man, talking non-stop from the corner of his mouth, hands deep in the pocket of his denim apron. He's not a customer: he occasionally passes Gus the sugar shaker, or squeezes the juice of lemons into a bowl. His hair is so blond it's almost white, a grown-out crop, unruly around the ears. His eyes are a contrasting dark brown, and that mouth, sloped at the corner, works on and on. In the noise of the deck, Nerissa cannot hear him. When the others have gone, eating their crêpes as they walk, it is her turn. Gus is already rolling the batter onto the plate.

"We're out of snails today. I can only do cheese. But Nick here has found a really good Stilton. It's very ripe—got a lovely rottenness about it."

The man in the apron, Nick, is still talking, but in barely a whisper. Surely Gus cannot hear him.

"Just lemon and sugar," says Nerissa, balancing on a barrel. "I'm Nerissa."

She extends a hand. The man's mouth stops moving, and he reaches out his bony fingers.

"Nick."

His voice is normal, not the whisper of before. He sounds antipodean. She wonders if it was her hearing, straining against the noise of the deck, the wash of the sea under everything.

"Nick's one of the chefs for Social. He's from New Zealand originally. A long way from home."

Nick smiles. She notes a white scar from nose to lip, a mouth crammed with teeth. His jaw is slightly angled. This makes sense of the way his words come through the edge of his mouth, as if he's smoking an invisible cigar.

"Nothing but sheep there." He laughs, but then seems regretful, as though he's insulted someone, and adds, "A beautiful place. I've not been there for years, but I do miss it."

Nerissa takes her crêpe, enjoying the gritty sugar and sharp lemon on her tongue. Nick and Gus step to one side and continue talking, looking at her from time to time as if including her in the conversation. She can only make out some words, most of them Gus's.

"It's not unlikely?" says Gus. "Everyone says that. Where's the evidence?"

"Accounts ... hear a lot more than you do ... almost everyone passing through ... don't imagine there's any harm ... on the other hand ... should just let him ..."

"Okay, okay. So what if there was? Why? You wouldn't have to hide."

"You might. All depends."

"Why don't we ask Nerissa? Perhaps she has some sense in her."

Nerissa gets up, shifting her barrel closer.

"It's ridiculous," says Gus, spreading his hands over the counter, "these rumours."

"Rumours of what?"

"A stowaway," says Nick. "Someone aboard, hiding."

Nerissa leans forwards, but tries not to look too eager. She keeps her knowledge of the graffiti to herself.

"See," says Gus, "she thinks you're an idiot too."

"I'm not the only one. People talk about it a lot."

"Of course they do. It's something for them to get excited about now they have begun to grow bored."

Nick rests on his elbows for a moment, watching Gus as he works a wet cloth around the hot plate. Steam rises up. There's a smell of scorched butter. Nick moves over to Nerissa and sits astride one of the barrels.

"I'll tell you the story, since you at least seem interested," he says, eyeing Gus, who snorts.

"Go ahead. Tell her about it. Make it entertaining now."

Nick ignores Gus and leans in.

"Listen, he doesn't believe anything he can't see with his own eyes, or prod with his fingers. But that doesn't mean it's not true. You must have heard stories about the stowaway already, no?"

Nerissa shrugs, shakes her head as she polishes off the crêpe. She slaps the sugar from her palms.

"That's because she's sensible, stays away from gossip," says Gus.

"Ah, like I say. Forget him. I know almost everyone here; they come through Social. You're not so familiar, a bit shy, maybe?"

He raises his eyebrows, but doesn't wait for a response.

"You learn a lot, listening to conversations. Everyone has a story. Something they lost, places they've been, the skills they're using on the ship that they've never used that way before. The rumour about the stowaway began a short while after we boarded. There's no smoke without fire. No wave without wind. Passengers were gossiping, saying they'd seen a figure hiding in the shadows, managing to live rough, scaring the girls at night. That he left his trash in the pipes. Bolted up service ladders if you called to him, if you asked who was there in the dark."

Nick pauses and lifts his head. "Hey, Gus, where's that coffee you're meant to be making me? And one for the lady too. All your broken promises!"

He laughs. "So, you want to know more?"

Gus rolls his eyes. Nerissa smiles, though she's feeling uneasy around this man with his long story and sideways manner of talking.

"I want to know more. Where have I been all these months, missing the drama?"

"Doing something useful," says Gus, handing them coffee. It's thick and hot. It tastes of chicory.

Nick blows on the steam, tapping the top of his barrel with one hand.

"So, he's a criminal, that's for sure," Nick begins again. "There's no prison on the ship as such. We might need something one day, but they certainly didn't want to start that way. He knew people would recognise him quick, but he was coming aboard; come hell or high water, he would save himself. And from that point on, he's hidden anywhere he can. Changes the way he looks by stealing clothes. Eats trash and leftovers. Moves around all the time. He's slept in the engine room. Even on the top deck, where none of us have been. He's tricksy. In his other life he was a house robber, a smart thief. That's why he can pick locks. Why he's agile. He chose the wrong house, one time. He didn't realise it belonged to the head of Green Media. It wasn't worth it. The only person in that day was the daughter, and he killed her. He'd never been a murderer before. Most think it was an accident. He was on the run from that point because he knew he'd be made an example of. But he was greedy, for sure. Could never get enough. Now he's living like a rat in a sewer, until they catch him. And they will."

"Sounds like a tall tale to me," says Gus. "Why don't we see anyone looking for him? Or telling the rest of us to be vigilant? Doesn't add up to me."

Nick slaps the barrel, jerks his head, angry that the spell of his story is broken.

"Gus, don't be naïve. They wouldn't tell us. They don't want ship-wide panic. Or a mob taking the law into their own hands. Why announce a killer is on the loose? Can you imagine? There's nowhere to go. No, they're searching for him. They do it at night."

He's silent for a moment, as if listening. The sounds of the market eddy around them. He stares at Nerissa.

"Maybe they already have him. That's more than likely. But the rumours are still going, from their original momentum."

"So you're not afraid of him?" asks Nerissa. She pictures the man hunkered in the gap at the end of the deck with a sharpened piece of silverware. Did he write the graffiti himself, in some show of defiance? Or has he been adopted as a hero?

"He's a thief gone wrong, nothing to fear unless you threaten him. He doesn't want to cause trouble here—just to survive. That's what I believe."

Nick finishes his coffee, closes his eyes.

"Know what I think, Nicholas?" says Gus, leaning his big body over the counter and grinning. "You tell a good story to impress the ladies. And that people like this story because we're all so well-behaved. Someone's got to be bad for us."

Nerissa laughs at the way Gus elongates the word "bad". She likes the banter between these two men, the way she cannot tell what's true and what's an act put on for her, which of the two of them is joking. It reminds her of messing around with Greg. She wonders if they've seen that graffiti in the nook in the deck, and spun the tale from there. Or if they planted the words themselves for the curious, to give the youngsters something to whisper about after school as the sun goes down.

"Thanks for the gossip," she says, slipping down from the barrel. "I feel much more in the loop."

She hands her plate and mug to Gus. Nick looks at her, his mouth a thin line, shoulders tense where he grips the barrel.

"You'll see," he says softly, almost a mumble.

Molloy

quivers in the widened-out end of the pipe. He looks through a grille, eyes darting over the scene beyond. He can't see what he wants. He shuffles, lifts one paw, then the next. He's colder now and wants to go through the grille and into the light. He bites the hard metal. It doesn't give. Beyond the grille he can see a group of people. They smell milky, musky, and acidic. That's how he knows they are teenagers, not adults. They are sitting in a circle, cross-legged, surrounded by shadows. There are two torches in the centre, casting weak, bluish beams of light. Molloy doesn't know it, but this is Deck Seven, at the edge of the engine room. It's late now. The students shouldn't be here. One of them, a girl with dark, unruly curls, is whispering. His device picks up her voice, while he stops, tasting the air.

"... he's really tall, too. He's got one blue eye and one brown. He's kind of beautiful. Like ugly-beautiful. And he's an artist. That's what I heard."

"And he sings?" Another girl, with skinny wrists and a low, masculine voice, leans forwards into the light.

"Yeah. He's got an old electric guitar with him. A Strat."

A boy, who smells particularly spicy to the Woolly Rat, coughs out a laugh, then quickly stifles it. Something mechanical clicks and begins to hum beneath the group's words.

"How can he do that without an amp?" says the boy.

The girl curls her lip. "It's not plugged in. He just strums it to remind himself. He has to be really quiet, anyway."

"The Stowaway is writing a manifesto. For when we land. For the new society we're going to have. It's all about people making cool art, and working together. About deciding what you want to study and stuff."

"I bet it's a bit more complicated than that."

The boy shifts and jogs his bent knee up and down. He picks at something on the decking. His face is flushed.

"I think it's crap," he says. "Bet he can't play. Bet he's just a coward. Why not show himself otherwise? To us, at least."

"Maybe he thinks we'd turn him in. He doesn't know what we think. That we think he's awesome."

The girl with the skinny wrists leans in again, the torchlight arching her brows.

"I'd go out with him," she says, at which the other girl bristles.

"He's too old for you. And anyway, you've never had a boyfriend."

She ignores her. "We could let him know. We could leave some sort of sign that tells him we support him. We want to be part of it. Marco from the other class says he knows him. He's been to the top deck with him. He's got photos. Came back with wet feet. So we could let him know—"

The dark girl interrupts, her voice rising with excitement, and then dipping into a whisper.

"They think he's dangerous. But they don't get it. I heard he left his parents to get on here. That he's only got a criminal record 'cause of a protest he went to. He's completely brilliant. So we've got to show support. We could post messages around the decks, write things on the walls and stairways."

"We don't know where he is, though."

"Doesn't matter. We put things up everywhere we can."

The boy brushes the dark girl's shoulder, where her sweater is slipping down. She doesn't notice. The skinny-wristed girl starts chewing the ends of her hair.

"What if we get caught?"

"Are you scared, Imogen?"

"Not really. But I don't want to get locked up somewhere."

The boy snorts. "Don't be lame. If we want to be part of this, we've got to take a risk or two. I like Darcy's idea about these messages. I'll do it."

He squares his shoulders, eyeing her for a reaction, which she doesn't offer. Her face is in shadow as she stands up, brushing dirt from her jeans.

"Right. So Tom can get some pens and maybe paint from school. And paper. You need to get into the cupboard. And steal gradually, so it isn't noticed. During breaks. And Immi, if you want, you can make posters, but we'll distribute them, if you're scared."

"I'm not scared," she says, eyes narrowing, a soft sob under her voice.

Molloy bites on the grille again, eager for their young voices, their sweet, sweaty scent. The bars rattle against his hard, square teeth. The group swirls around at the noise, scrabbling to switch their torches off.

"Shhh!"

There are some other whispers Molloy experiences only as low murmurs. Then a scrambling against the boards. The sound of the huge engine, pulsing in the dark. A flicker of torchlight in the distance. Molloy's nose darts wetly out through the bars. The scent is gone. Now he picks up something else: boiled cabbage, ripe cheese, coming from the left. He stretches, pushing his back legs against the cool metal of the pipe, and slips away.

Captain Holmes

Nerissa cuts the thread on the cat's wound, and runs her hand along his fur.

"Hiya, Herm. What's happening?"

He's holding two mugs and a carefully balanced stack of biscuits.

"Just thought you might want something. How did this go?" He gestures to the cat, still flopped out.

"Good. I always worry about the anaesthetics here; this monitor is a bit old. But it's not so bad for all that. This chap is a pet of one of the families. I want to give him back in one piece. He ate something that wasn't really edible."

She lifts a plastic jar up that contains a large glass sphere. It is delicately painted blue and green. Herman takes it from her and holds it to the light.

"What is it?"

"I don't know, to be honest." She sips her tea. "I can't figure it out. It's like a huge marble. It looks like it probably belonged to something else at some point. It seems too big to be a toy."

She lifts the floppy cat and takes him to one of the cages stacked along the edge of the room. He'll recover here.

"I need to go down later. Look at the lions."

"They're okay. I've got a lot of horse manure collecting down there. I had some students mucking out today."

"That's great. Did they seem interested?"

"Yes. One of them, anyway. He asked a few questions about their pens, how we exercise them. He really wanted to know what will happen when we reach land. If, when we let them out, they'll go and eat each other."

Nerissa laughs into her tea. Her face softens for a moment, and she says, "I only wish we knew when we will land. I asked the steward if I might be able to get a meeting with the captain."

Herman says nothing, crunching his biscuit. Nerissa has learned that this means he's thinking.

After a moment, he says, "Some stewards are coming this week, to take the manure to the Garden Deck."

"But what do you think about the captain?"

"I don't know, Boss. We are due an announcement. When he gave us the instructions, he seemed to think the animals were important."

That was true. A message over the monitors for each section of the ship. For each task, each role. Nerissa and Herman had their own message shortly after they boarded, transmitted into the lab, while they were still working out what equipment they had, still getting to know one another. Captain Holmes's elegant face had appeared, speaking to them.

"First of all, I must apologise for the recorded message. I'm trying to be efficient."

Nerissa had noticed his navy blue jacket and some symbol she had never seen before, a flower or perhaps a hand, pinned to the lapel. A slight flush spread up his neck.

"I will regularly make announcements to the whole vessel, but these future messages will be live. I've recorded this especially for Nerissa Crane and Herman Hart."

He leant forwards at this point, as if to get a closer look at them. It felt uncanny.

"Nerissa Crane, no doubt you know more about your role than I do. We're lucky to have someone with your expertise. I felt it was important to bring some live specimens aboard the *Baleen*, although there are those"—at this point his eyes shifted, for a millisecond, to his right—"that disagree. Yes, resources are at a premium. But we don't know what has survived. There may be creatures on the high ground, but we have no idea which, or how many. Those animals we have are those we could save, from zoos and even private collectors, so forgive us that they don't represent the species we might have saved, and that our facilities leave something to be desired. We also want those aboard to know how special these creatures are, in their difference from us. You two are here to educate, and to care for these precious specimens. Yourself and Mr Hart will need to be frugal, to work together with the crop team. But we are a small vessel and will not be at sea long. That is the hope."

He leaned back then, again looking at things that were beyond the frame of the camera. Through a porthole and at the horizon, perhaps. Or he was simply thinking of what to say next.

"If you need anything, don't hesitate to ask the stewards. There is also a list—I assume you have seen it—of people who deal with certain resources. We'll muddle through. In the meantime, I leave it to you. Take good care of them all. Keep them from harm."

After that, there were live messages that crackled onto all the monitors on all decks, once or twice a week. Captain Holmes's charming face appeared with its half-smile to tell everyone about a new menu in the cafeteria, to encourage more vendors to open stalls, to announce new classes at the school. The messages were tailing off now. They had not had one for two weeks. Herman said it was because everyone was settled in. They had worked things out, in those early weeks. Scavenging for the things they needed, devising a system with the Garden Deck, providing manure and getting grain in return. She and Herman had been wary of each other at first. Herman was shy, as well as gruff and sad. She knows that most passengers don't want to think about the time before. This blank, out-of-joint situation is an ideal one in which to forget. But, lately, they have begun to swap stories.

They lost many animals in the first month. The change of environment, the shock, the microbes living imperceptibly in the fusty air, the closeness of species that would normally never meet, all these contributed to the deaths. A few turned on their own young, as they would never normally do. Nerissa would find the mothers, mouths bloodied, bewildered at their own acts, the soft bodies of their young ripped open. For some there was no chance of mating again. Herman was more squeamish than her, more upset. She noticed he would be quiet for hours after these incidents and tidy anything but the bodies. She did that herself. Sometimes she felt a trace of warmth in the remains. Most bodies were burned, or fed to others where possible. But when the African elephant went, like a great tangle of fallen oak, a team had to be called to haul her up the decks and over the side. Nerissa and Herman had watched at the porthole to see her come floating down into the darkening green. They stood shoulder to shoulder, as if at a funeral, until her shadow receded beneath them.

The cat is coming round and mews softly, testing out his small voice.

"Can you take him up, Herm, to Deck Six? Room 112."

"Sure, I'll go after my tea."

"And how are the mice today?"

"We've got a new brood. And some rabbits too. Shall I do the usual?"

With some of the small, breeding animals, a quarter of the babies are kept. Herman portions them out for Nerissa. It is she who feeds their squirming bodies to the snakes and crocodiles. He cannot watch their tiny deaths, the bulge as they pass down the greater creature's throat.

Summer Storms

Nerissa must have been five, maybe six years old when it happened. The rain was smashing against the panes of all the windows, and she heard the great, angry barrels of thunder. The clouds "rubbing each other up the wrong way," her dad always said. She wasn't afraid, but excited. She longed to go out on such days, with her wellies and mac, to see the jagged trails of lightning plugging into the hills, earthing on the masts of the office blocks to the western skyline. She wanted to feel the fresh, cool rain on her skin, to taste the minerals in it. It was late afternoon, mid-summer and blue-dark. Her dad was in his workshop, head under the bonnet of a car.

"Let me go out," she would have said, playfully tugging his grease-stained jeans.

"No, little Lollipop, you'll get struck by lightning, then there'll be nothing left of you but your welly-boots and the end of your nose."

She squealed as he tickled her in the armpit. Her father had bright blue eyes and a shock of silver hair, as if he had once been struck by lightning and it still crackled within him. His eyes crinkled when he smiled, and he always had black grime underneath his fingernails. He was a mechanic and spent his days in the workshop repairing vintage cars for wealthy customers who still got a thrill from a diesel engine. He had been an engineer, but lost his job when the machines took over, as he put it. He wore overalls most of the time and was thin, with a little belly.

Hot, stark blue days without a wisp of cloud were followed by those storms. But this day was different from the others, and some of the details were indelible. She'd wandered up and down the unfinished, slippery wooden stairs of their old house, trailing her knitted rabbit, looking for something to do, when she'd made a discovery. Between the second and third floors of the house, there was a landing that stopped abruptly under a sloped window, and in the gap there was a cupboard. It was full of old tins of paint, off-cuts of wood, cardboard boxes. Nerissa liked to curl up in there with a comic and her knitted rabbit, pretending to read by looking at the pictures and guessing the story, while listening to the storm.

On one of these afternoons she heard a scratching sound. It was faint but persistent, and it came from the corner of the dusty cupboard. She imagined all manner of things: fairies, tiny burglars, a big spider wearing eight shoes. But she was not afraid. She padded down to her bedroom with the spirit of an explorer, to get a torch, and pushed its light into the dusty shadows of the cupboard. There was something white and furry in there, its flank moving lightly with its breath. It was warm-blooded with polished eyes looking back at her and a set of whiskers quivering like the strings of a miniature violin. She stretched her hand out to it, and it shrank back into the shadows, where even her small fingers could not reach it. At some point, she took the creature some food: chocolate from her secret store, and a piece of bread torn from a loaf at dinner and stuffed in her pocket. She coaxed the creature with a trail of these delicacies and saw its neat, nude mouth, its wet eyes, and those trembling whiskers. She touched its white fur as it chewed the bread. She thought it was a mouse, like the ones people turned into in her story books. She knows now that it was too large and tame for that and must have been a rat. Whilst her mother and father worked, she kept the rat a secret, visiting him with scraps on those wild, rainy days. She didn't understand names well at that age and simply called him "Friendly".

Although her dad told her not to, if she couldn't stand the boredom any more, she would climb the highest flight of stairs and visit her mother's attic.

“Your mother’s the brains,” her dad would often say, to which her mother would bump him on the arm and say, “Don’t be daft, Caleb.”

The attic room seemed like the largest in the house, despite the sloping sides of the roof. Perhaps it was the fact that the windows gave the most open view of the sky beyond the rooftops, the way she could see uninterrupted chunks of it changing colour through the day. Her mother spent most of her time up there in the summer, and in the winter, many of her evenings, after she came back from the university. Nerissa crept to the top step and waited there. Her mother would usually be so absorbed she wouldn’t notice her at first. Her mother’s name was Leonora, and Nerissa still remembers that her father would say it in a particular way, a way no one else did, with a slight growl on the “r”. Leonora had soft, dark skin and a mass of curls she’d wear in their natural state, but wrapped in a scarf to keep them out of her work. Nerissa has not inherited her mother’s rounded breasts and hips, and her skin is much lighter, but her hair has a trace of that springy coarseness. There were two vast tables in the attic and a big bookshelf. Nerissa remembers jars and bottles, heavy books, the blue glow of a computer. All forbidden to her touch. Her mother would either be writing notes, typing, or frowning over some specimen with a microscope. She still does not know exactly what her mother researched, but it was some scientific niche that no one seemed interested in, and the pressure to discover, to prove, to publish, was always there.

“What are you doing, my love?” she would say, looking up when she finally noticed Nerissa’s presence.

Nerissa would climb the final step and stand at the mouth of the attic, the smell of chlorine in the air.

“I want you to play, Mama.”

Leonora would frown, pull off her latex gloves with a snap, and come to the stairs to touch Nerissa’s cheek.

“Now, my baby, you know I’ve got to finish this. So we can stay living here, where we like to live. You know that, right? I promise I'll come out with you on Saturday. If it doesn't rain. We'll go to the woods—how's that?"

"Okay."

"Okay. So, an hour until dinner."

And at dinner she would get her love, get to watch her stirring the pots, putting her peat-brown arm into the crook of her father's pale, silver-haired arm, watching them both framed against the blueness outside the kitchen window.

One afternoon, when the rain had not yet come but the clouds hung low and sticky, Nerissa went to her cupboard, a cool and dark escape. Friendly was not there as he usually was, snuffling for his scraps. But something else, a timorous chirping, came from the very back of the cupboard. She smelt something that reminded her of her father's work clothes under the steam of the iron. Her torch illuminated the nest and the tiny, naked babies with their fused-shut eyes writhing inside it. Friendly was not a "he" after all. She was so thrilled she ran upstairs to the attic to give up her secret. Surely even her mother's work was not as important as Friendly's new family?

When she reached the top step, her mother was there as usual, bent over her work. There was something spread out on the table, something stretched and white she could make no sense of at first. Breathless from the steps, she watched her mother bring a silver implement down, pull at a strand, wipe something red, remove something. Nerissa crept into the room, not asking for permission. Her voice was trapped inside her ribcage. She drew close to the table, saw the little beads of two shiny eyes, now staring blankly with their light out, the whiskers straight and still like wires, the white fur open, stretched out, the body red inside. Red and full of bones. Her mother only looked up when she screamed.

"What happened to the babies?" asks Herman, sipping his tea, his russet eyebrows knitted together. They have taken to telling each other stories like this only recently. With little to make new memories with, the old ones are emerging more often.

"They died, I think, without their mother. I have a memory of them in their nest: desiccated little bones. But I don't know; I might have imagined it. It occurred to me later that what I saw my mother dissecting may not have been the same rat at all. It makes little sense if you think about it."

"Aye," says Herman, "unless it escaped from her for a time, and it was always intended for ... Nasty, though, to see that, when you were a tiny thing." He pauses to splash his mug out over the sink. "What happened to them, your parents, I mean?"

Nerissa thinks of her mother that winter, her belly taut and rounded under the fabric of her woollen dresses. Her usually warm-brown skin took on a grey sheen, and there were dark circles under her eyes. The snow was too deep to get in or out for a time.

"She got sick. It was something genetic, triggered by her pregnancy. She'd died by spring, before the wildflowers came up. The baby died too, before it was born. My dad took me away from that house, a long way from that town. I don't even know where it was. We just carried on without them somehow."

"Until?"

"Until I went to vets' college. He just sort of drifted away, without her to anchor him. No one else would do. I only saw him when he visited. I loved to see him. And then he died, about a year after I graduated. I wasn't with him. I was away when it happened."

"I'm sorry," says Herman. "You've lost a lot."

She rubs a hand through the back of her hair, swallowing hard.

"No more than anyone else here," she says, giving Herman a half-smile.

"Have you thought of going to one of the 'Letting Go' ceremonies?" he says, looking away from her and tidying some glass beakers, lining them up neatly at the edge of the sink.

"Really, Herman, don't those things strike you as a bit weird?"

"I don't know. I went to one the other night. Just hung back, really, and watched. It was sort of uplifting. I might do it properly next time. Everyone is very kind."

Nerissa sighs. "I'll think about it."

She swings down the ladder, back to the animals, the survivors, to be surrounded by their warm breath, their living smells.

Molloy

travels up, gripping the indentations inside the rough pipework. Flashes of light from above. Glimmers of sound. Voices rising and fading as he moves. Shouts, giggles, moans. The smell of salt drifts down. Then it is pitch-black. Fingers of light coming up from below. His paws are on a silver mesh. Cool air on his belly. Molloy smells sweet milk and graphite. The device attached to him takes in children holding tablets, scrolling with their fingers, and some reading from crinkled books. It picks up their high voices.

"What did he look like?" chirps one.

"Well, he had a beard," comes the reply.

"A big one?"

"Yes, I think so."

"And he found some islands?" says another, shuffling closer.

"Yes, he did."

"And a turtle?"

"It would have been called a tortoise. But yes. A really big one. Well, more than one. And he found they could grow very old."

"Because they took their time about things?"

A muffled laugh. Molloy moves away. Everyone is too far down. He has a vague fear that he might fall. In the next pipe he finds a ragged hole leading out onto the deck. This is a storage section on the Garden Deck. Panels of wood separate it. He smells earth, shoots and buds, a peat he doesn't recognise. The camera picks up a shoe at an odd angle, twisting into the ground. The bottom of a leg. Then another. Two more, laces neatly tied. Deep, furtive voices. Molloy cannot see the grass he can smell.

He slips behind a spade, knocking the top of the camera. The image judders, and then clears.

"We only need a little more. For the edge of the square."

"We won't be caught?"

"No. And anyway, Antoinette said we could. It's not being used for anything."

They are scooping from a small pile of yellow sand. Two men, one much older than the other, their backs stooped. The way they smell, of new sweat, Molloy doesn't want to go near them. He shifts around, tasting for the earth and grass. It is behind this wooden panel. So he begins to gnaw.

Animals

The soft breathing of creatures in the near-dark. Only a deep blue filters in from the portholes down here in Deck Twelve. Nerissa pads along the narrow gangway between enclosures. The shadows of sleeping animals, their warm breath misting into the air. Their musky scent. Rabbits, wide awake, their eyes glistening, whiskers like trembling threads. Her own eyes adjust to the dark. She makes out the muscular flank of a horse, glossy where it lies on its side. Nerissa likes to come down here at night, to switch off her torch, to sense the life pulsing around her. As usual, the sea itself is blank, but with a soupy, dusty look to it. It is odd to see the confined life in here, and so little outside. An empty sea. Is it so toxic now that nothing may live? Will everything land-dwelling, which loves the soil, dust, and grass, be forever down here, watching for life to show itself in the dark?

She moves to a small anteroom, portioned off from the mammals. She switches her torch back on; little natural light filters in here. The edges of glass tanks rise up in the torch's beam. Insects of many kinds. Small amphibians just slipping into their artificial pools to hide from her. A praying mantis is poised on a branch, like a clockwork, his prominent eyes fixed on her, his angular body absolutely still. Still as a photograph.

Graduation

Nerissa excelled at veterinary college, spending her days engrossed in textbooks, tracing the anatomies of all kinds of creatures. Something in her wanted to make sense of the white rat she'd seen opened up on her mother's lab bench. She wanted to understand its inner workings so that she might know how to put it back together. She listened attentively to every lecture, dissected virtual creatures on screens with perfect accuracy and declined drinks with her classmates in favour of her books or all-nighters in the lab. When it came to graduation, she gained the highest marks in her class. She remembers the day, adjusting her gown and mortar board in her tiny kitchen mirror. Her dad put his hand on her shoulder. He had come to visit, especially for graduation. He smiled, and the edges of his blue eyes crinkled. He didn't smile often.

"Leonora would be proud," he said, pronouncing her name in that growling way for the first time in ages.

"I know, Dad. Do I look ridiculous?"

"You look great. Just don't trip on the podium, and all will be fine. I can't believe you're getting this special prize, that you're the tops."

Nerissa grinned at him from the mirror, her mortar board slightly too big and slipping to the left. The work had paid off, and she was going to use her prize money for a trip to Borneo.

"You sure you want to go all that way?" her dad said, as the tram crept up the hill to the university hall. "Just to hang out with gorillas?"

"They're orangutans, Dad," she said, sure he was teasing her. "And I really do. I need an adventure after all that studying. I want to work with real animals more."

Her dad was silent for a moment, gripping the strap in the tram as it came to the top of the hill. Then he said, "People of the forest," and smiled gently at her. She looped her arm into his, and they stepped off together.

After graduation, the hall was full, loud with graduates chatting, holding their mortar boards in one hand, a glass of fizz in the other. Nerissa's father stood a little way off with her favourite lecturer, the imposing Professor Hughes. She talked with her classmates about their plans.

"I'm going to a practice in Aberdeen," said Verity, a girl with a moon-face and a worried look. "It's a good spot. Really safe at the moment. Are you sure about the Borneo thing? What if you catch something, or get bitten by a snake?"

"I'll be all right, Verity," Nerissa said and laughed. She was about to say more when a tall, pale woman stepped out of the crowd and touched her on the shoulder. She had a sleek helmet of lush red hair, bright green eyes framed precisely by shaped brows, and full lips.

"Excuse me for interrupting you, girls," she said in a sonorous voice. Nerissa could not place the accent. "I wonder if I might have a word with Ms Crane?"

Nerissa felt suddenly scruffy, the heavy collar of her graduation gown listing to one side, her hair flattened by the band on her mortar board.

"Sure," she said, putting down her glass to take the woman's long, outstretched fingers.

"I'm Dr Mortimer. Esther."

"I'm—"

"Yes, I know your name. Nerissa. Because of the prize, of course. Your professors are impressed by your talents."

Nerissa looked at her shoes, polished that morning, and touched the back of her head. When she looked up, Esther was smiling warmly at her. Verity had wandered away, never keen for others to have attention, and was talking to a boy from their class.

"I have an offer to make you, Nerissa. A job offer. If you're interested. Do you want to chat outside, where it's quiet?"

There were lemon and fig trees in the courtyard of the university, and their gorgeous, ripe perfume hung in the humid air. Esther took something long and white from a case in her pocket, and lit it.

"What is that?"

"Ah,"—she smiled—"a cigarette. I suppose not many young people have seen one. Do you want to try? I won't tell if you won't."

Nerissa looked around the empty courtyard, and through the doorway into the busy hall, her heart thrumming. "No, no thanks." The strange, burnt smell caught in her nostrils. It was not unpleasant.

"Contraband. I know. We all have our weaknesses." Esther drew the cigarette away from her painted lips and exhaled with satisfaction.

"I work at the Mithras Institute," she said, "in Istanbul. We are doing very special things there. With animals, finding ways to conserve them, make them stronger to withstand our environment, which we both know is becoming hostile. Saving species. Professor Hughes tells me such things are close to your heart."

"Yes," said Nerissa. She felt both pride and panic rising in her chest.

"Well," Esther began, as she flicked the cigarette to the ground, barely smoked, and crushed its ember with her heel, "I'd like to offer you a job with us. Entry level at first, but good pay. You'd work your way up. A flat to live in. Istanbul is a vibrant city."

Nerissa wondered at first if Esther had mistaken her for another student. But she knew she was top of her class. She glanced over at Professor Hughes. What had he been saying about her?

"I don't know what to say. I'm so flattered." Nerissa felt the heat in her cheeks. Her words seemed naïve and ridiculous. Esther turned to face her, looking at her intently.

"Each year, I consider the top person graduating from this course. Most years, I don't offer anyone a job."

"It's just that, I have a plan, to go to Borneo, to Sabangau National Park. It's all arranged. I've wanted to ..."

Nerissa thought Esther would be offended, but she smiled warmly again, squeezed her arm, and said, "Of course. Take my card. Get in touch if you change your mind. And just call me if—"

"Nerissa?" Her father stood in the doorway to the courtyard, late afternoon light sparkling in his white hair.

"Dad, this is Esther Mortimer, she's—"

"Mr Crane." Esther stretched out her hand. He took it, unsmiling.

"Call me Caleb," he said. He frowned as Esther spoke.

"I was just chatting to your talented daughter."

"That she is," he said, his expression softening. "She's great."

"I've told her, if she's looking for a job, to get in touch."

"Oh, right. And who ... ?

"I'm from the Mithras Institute."

She passed him another card. On the front was a stylised image of a bull, on the back an address and number. His eyes flicked over it, and he slipped it into his suit pocket.

"Well, she's going to Borneo, and then, who knows? I want her to have some adventures. She's worked so hard."

He wrapped his big arm around Nerissa's shoulder, and she relaxed beneath it.

"Come on," he said, turning away, "I promised you a pint in the Crow and Lion, as I recall. Good to meet you, Ms Mortimer."

"It's actually Doctor, but you can call me Esther." She opened her palm in a quick wave, and Nerissa followed her father back through the crowds, pushing the card Esther had given her deep into her pocket. It would be three years before she looked at the card again.

Gus

Nerissa wakes, her head against straw, a smell like a late August from that other life itching in her nostrils. Violet light filters in ribbons over the jigsawed back of a tortoise. It chews slowly on a leaf, watching her from the edge of its enclosure. Herman leans over her, not getting too close, a bucket slack in one hand, the other tentatively touching her shoulder.

"Did you sleep here? Are you all right?" He looks tired.

"I'm fine." She leans up stiffly, spittle dry on her cheek. She's never fallen asleep here. Herman gives a half-smile, resting the bucket down without letting go of its handle.

"You're not ill? If you are, we can see the Doc. I know he's only a medical student, but he's okay. I saw him about my throat."

"No, I just couldn't sleep, so I came down here. I must have—"

"You go back up to your bed and sleep more. Or get some tea. I've only got a little feeding left to do."

"Okay."

He takes her elbow as she stands. She can feel him watching her as she climbs the ladder back into her workroom. She's careful not to slip.

After a shower she looks at herself in the fluorescent glow of her tiny mirror, tucking the tufts of her grown-out crop behind her ears. For a moment, she can think of nothing at all, as if her mind were that uninhabited sea. Her lips are cracked and dry again. She rubs petroleum jelly on them. She dresses in jeans, struggling with the top button, then slips on her plimsolls and a striped long-sleeved T-shirt, as if she were going somewhere, and heads for Deck Five.

Gus is at his *Crêperie* as usual, mixing the batter with his big arm in long strokes. He greets her with a broad smile.

"We have prawns today. Freshwater."

"Ah, yes. Herman said they were ready."

"You want some?"

"No, thank you. Just plain today."

Gus's brow wrinkles as he spreads the batter around the crackling plate. It deepens to creamy yellow and curls up at the edges.

"She is a little bit down in the dumps today?"

"I'm all right. Just a little bored."

He flaps the crêpe over, folds it onto a tin dish, and passes it to her. Nerissa stands and leans against a metal barrel.

"Ah. It is the worst thing. After the survival: the boredom. The desire for a desire. But you never come to Social …"

Nerissa is not really bored but does not want, or cannot find a way to, describe how she actually feels. How she has felt since she woke up amongst the animals.

"You know what you need?" Gus leans over the counter so that she sees the fine smile-lines at the corners of his lips and the dark edging to his irises.

"To go to Social, I know. I just can't take all those people sometimes, you know?"

"Not that. No. But, as my wife says, 'a pampering.'"

Nerissa grins at this odd suggestion of the old world. Standing here, leaning against a barrel, her battered plimsolls on the bare-boarded deck. She thinks of spas, pedicures, saunas. Remembers her girlfriends sipping neon-coloured cocktails. Fluffy white dressing gowns. Face-packs cracking on their laughing faces.

"You may laugh, Dr Crane, but go and see my wife. Laundry Deck. She knows what ladies need. A haircut, for one thing. Look," he says and reaches to gently ruffle her hair, "like un hérisson. A hedgehog."

Perhaps it is the light touch, the big, warm hand when she has had no tender contact for weeks. Or the memory of Greg's words about her haircut. Sharp tears stick in her throat and burn up behind her eyes. A flash of dismay crosses Gus's face. He opens his mouth, but she quickly says, "You're right. I'll go. It will do me some good, I'm sure." Twisting on her heel, she leaves her half-eaten crêpe on its tin plate.

He calls after her, "My wife's name is Marie."

Beachcombing

Nerissa's hair used to be a long mass of curls, looser than her mother's, which she plaited or braided. She rarely got it cut, but when she did, she'd go to an old school friend who worked in the salon tucked away from the seafront: *Beachcombing*. She'd get her nails done too—cherry red, pale lilac, soft pink. Such things don't matter to her now. She saw this friend, Cara, at other times—out for drinks with the girls, sipping neon cocktails in bars with floors damp and seaweedy from the latest flood. She never imagined these friends would just be gone, that she would never laugh with them again.

"So, what's this guy like, Riss?" said Cara, teasing out Nerissa's hair and combing it down the length of her back. Cara had glossy, straight hair that she dyed a different colour every month. On this day it was purple.

"What guy?" Nerissa saw herself blush in the salon mirror.

"I know you. You've got that thing about you when you're into someone. Come on, spill."

Nerissa smiled. Her friend knew her too well. Cara took her over to the basin and tipped her head back. The warm water rolled over Nerissa's scalp.

"Too hot?"

"No, perfect." Nerissa closed her eyes as Cara massaged the apple-scented shampoo into her hair.

"Okay, so I met someone on that trip last year."

"I knew it."

"And, well, you know, after Dad and everything."

Cara rubbed deeper and Nerissa's scalp prickled.

"Mmm. So?"

"Well, I left it. And then he got in touch. We've been seeing each other a bit, you know. I think I like him."

"Oh, come on, you have to give me more."

Nerissa talked over the whoosh of water and hairdryers. "He's exciting. Has some life in him."

"Bet he does."

"Stop it. It's true. It's almost as though he doesn't think anything bad will happen. The floods will stop."

"And you believe that bullshit?"

Nerissa opened her eyes and looked up at her friend, who stared down, her blue eyes narrow.

"It's not that he says it—I'm sure he knows things aren't good—but he lives like it will be okay."

"Well, maybe it will," said Cara softly, wrapping a towel around Nerissa's head. "Back to the mirror."

Nerissa eyed herself in the salon mirror whilst Cara towelled off her hair. If she looked at her reflection for too long, it grew strange, as if she'd never seen herself before.

"Tell me more." Cara snipped the ends of Nerissa's hair.

"He's nice-looking in a sort of old-fashioned way. He's a photographer. He travels a lot. Nothing seems to faze him. You know me, I worry a lot."

"I don't think you do. You're just cautious, that's all."

"I think I should be less cautious. I like the idea. Be a bit wild. Not always have my head in a book."

Cara rolled her eyes. "Honey, you're not a wild one. It doesn't suit you. You're too nice. I was surprised you went to the jungle."

"It was the rainforest," said Nerissa, a shot of temper in her voice. "I loved it there."

She thought then, but didn't speak, of the final days that forced her home. The sheets of metallic-looking rain. The thick darkness. The cracking sounds in the trees as their riverboat left by stealth to take them from danger.

“Dad wanted me to go out there, experience the world a bit. I was sheltered growing up.”

“He loved you, is all,” said Cara, pausing in her snipping to look at Nerissa’s reflection. Then she combed back her damp hair. “If you’re so wild, let’s cut this all off!”

“No way. Never. Not the hair. Never the hair, Cara,” Nerissa squealed, then giggled.

“Listen, I want to meet this crazy boy. Make sure he’s good enough for you. Those crazy ones seem good at first, but ...”

Cara had dealt with her fair share of unsuitable men; Nerissa had thought her jealous. She now can’t remember Cara and Greg ever meeting. Surely that would have been fun; why can’t she remember it? They must have met again, Cara and her, for drinks with the girls even when things got a bit worse. But nothing remains in her memory now. It has dissolved away.

Haircut

There are no quarters on Deck Four. It is a service deck, where much of the domestic work goes on. Part of the engine forms one side of it: a coppery-bloomed, bolted wall with a thick sheet of glass in front to protect people from its hot surface. There are large, vertical pipes to negotiate and puffs of steam fogging the portholes. The floor beneath Nerissa is part metal, part slatted wood. A narrow section of the deck opens out into an oval room following the curved shape of the *Baleen*. The entrance is thick with humidity, and inside, it is piled high with washing, dirty and clean, steaming, soft. Several women work quickly: folding, ironing, loading into large, mismatched tubs. There is a smell of cheap soap that takes Nerissa back, suddenly, to her parents' house. And another scent, private, musky, seeping through. She stands awkwardly in the doorway until someone turns: the girl with the red-blonde dreadlocks she has seen working as a vendor on Deck Five. Her cheeks and chest are flushed and freckled. Her eyelashes are almost white. She drops a hand to her hip.

"Can I help?"

"Err. I'm looking for Marie."

"Marie is out back." She gestures behind her with her thumb, but Nerissa can't see where she means. Everything is piled high with cloth, as if the room were constructed from it. She carefully walks past the women. One or two look up at her. None smile. One is pressing with an old steam iron, disappearing intermittently behind great white clouds. At the far end, around the back of a pile of children's clothes, is a narrow white door with a glass panel.

"Just go in," someone calls through the steam.

Nerissa clicks open the door. Another anteroom, triangle-shaped and porthole-free, lies beyond. There are three chairs and a large mirror surrounded by light bulbs like the kind from a theatre dressing-room (though none of the bulbs are lit). A small, plump woman with sleek, dark hair and feline eyes turns and grins at her.

"I'm Marie. Gus told me you might come."

Her accent is like Gus's, but her voice is sonorous and high. She gestures to one of the chairs in front of the mirror. Her movements are fluid and quick. As Nerissa sits, she sees the back corner of the room reflected in the mirror. Four other women are playing cards at a trestle table. One is painting her nails carefully, whilst concealing what Nerissa can see is a winning hand.

"Don't mind them. They're on their break. Do you have any green tokens?"

"Yes." Nerissa hands her two green 'leisure' tokens. She feels flushed and light-headed, willing to do whatever this woman tells her, as long as she can rest.

"One is enough. I'll get you some tea." Marie places a towel around Nerissa's shoulders. Nerissa barely feels her touch. Then Marie wanders to the back corner of the room.

One of the women around the table is watching Nerissa in the mirror. She has a high mass of chestnut curls sitting atop her head, and short, pearl-painted nails. She might be about sixty-five. She lays her cards down for a moment and takes a sip of something tea-coloured from her glass. The other women look at her.

"Are you playing or what?" says one of the others.

The woman clears her throat and answers, "Just thinking about it."

Marie is back with a steaming cup, which she places in front of Nerissa. For a moment the women and their card game are obscured by her reflection. Marie smiles at Nerissa in the mirror, spraying a mist of water on her hair and combing it through.

"You'd like a trim? Tidy this all up. With short styles, you know they need cutting more often."

"Yes, I suppose. Thank you." Looking at herself with damp hair, under violet-tinged light, Nerissa notices how lean her face has become, the shadows beneath her eyes. The chestnut-haired woman is visible again and has angled her chair towards them.

"Marie, introduce us." She has the husky voice of a smoker. Marie catches Nerissa's eye in the mirror.

"This is Nerissa Crane, ship's vet. Nerissa, this is Pam. And Beryl, Suzanne, and Shirley."

The other women smile at her, cards still poised in their hands. Beryl has a chic, grey bob and a lick of liner over each eye. She looks the oldest, perhaps seventy. She says: "Marie gives a wonderful pedicure. I suppose people think these things aren't important anymore. But it's what keeps me going, to be honest. I used to have a whole wardrobe of the most fabulous clothes. I kept things for years."

Marie is guiding the scissors deftly around Nerissa's ears. She hears the soft snip as tufts float to the ground.

"No grey yet. And you're quite dark, so that is lucky."

The women have turned back to their game, but before long the winning hand goes down and they let out little gasps of mock-horror. The chestnut-headed Pam turns to Nerissa again.

"You look after all the animals, then?"

"Yes. Well, apart from a few that are peoples' pets, cats or whatever. I only see those if they get ill."

"What kinds of animals have you got down there? Are they dangerous?" asks Shirley, a plump, dark-skinned lady who looks younger than the others. Nerissa remembers the steward's words before she speaks.

"No, nothing dangerous. Not like that. And they are all secure in different cages and enclosures."

"They can't like it much," says Suzanne, who is slipping something stronger into her tea, "all cooped up together."

"Not much, no. But it's not forever."

Marie moves around to cut the back. Nerissa feels her warm breath on her neck. The door opens, letting in a blast of hot air, and the dread-locked girl, pink-cheeked, strides into the room.

"There's iced tea in the back, Rachel."

"Thanks."

She returns quickly, gulping it down, watching the others.

"You know what I heard?" says Pam. "You know that stowaway—"

"Not that again, Nan." Rachel smiles.

"Look, my lovely, everyone's talking about him."

"Okay, so what's the story this time? He's an alien? An artificial human experiment?"

Pam wrinkles her nose, clears her throat.

"I love having a granddaughter," she says, "don't you all know it. But she's not too respectful, is she?"

"She's a grownup, really," says Beryl.

"That's as may be. But she never listens to her poor old Nan. I might be wrinkly, for sure I am, but I've seen a thing or two. A few stories that would make your hair curl. Well, maybe not yours, Beryl."

They all laugh, quivery but deep, fruity laughs. Rachel grins.

"How about you, Marie? You're sensible. Do you believe in all this stowaway stuff?"

Marie is combing the front of Nerissa's fringe, then cutting across the comb to create shape around her face.

"Gus tells me a few stories he hears from the deck. I don't believe them. For one thing, no two stories are exactly the same; at least the stowaway isn't the same in them. For another, why hide? Except if you've done something really bad. Perhaps it's someone a bit different or shy. Just keeping to themselves. That's what I think. Or it's imaginary. Everyone sees what they want to see, don't they?"

"Well, what about mine?" says Pam, her voice husky and excited. "Nerissa made me think of it, my encounter."

"I want to hear," says Suzanne, topping her tea up again.

"Let me dry Nerissa's hair first. Make another pot."

Nerissa can't hear anything above the dryer, but she watches as the women jostle and fuss in the cupboards, laughing, touching one another's arms. Her hair dries with bounce and a gentle curl at the front. It looks like it did a few months ago, but her face does not match it.

"There, that's better, don't you think?"

"Yes, thank you."

"Stay a while. Hear Pam's ridiculous story. I'll get another tea for you."

Nerissa feels the echo of Greg's warm fingertips, just for a second, resting against her neck.

Laundry

They sit around the trestle table on folding chairs, with mugs of tea. Pam meets each of their gazes as she talks.

"I was here late one night," she says, "sorting the underwear. I got something muddled up—you know how I do—and I put two batches of undies together that belonged to different families. I thought, good Lord, that won't ever do. I wanted to put it right before morning. I had some music on, turned down low, and only the light on in the laundry room—"

"Goodness," interrupts Beryl, "I would be spooked right away. All those white sheets in the dead of night!"

Pam gives her a look, sips her tea, and continues,

"Well, there I was, folding and sorting and stacking when I hear a *fwump!*"

"A what?"

"You know, a *fwump*, a sort of soft thud. And I saw a stack of laundry on the far side just tip over."

Marie leans back in her chair. Beryl opens her mouth, but Pam says, "Just let me go on. I'll tell you what happened.

"So I thought it had just gone over, because it was stacked so high. I didn't worry. I carried on. I remember because Creamy O'Hagan was on the radio. You know I love him. I whistled along a bit. I kept going. Thinking of a cuppa and my bed. Then it happened again—*fwump*—over the other side. A fresh stack of sheets slid over. I was annoyed, really, more than anything; they'd been pressed and folded. I went over there. It's darker in the corners at night. But I saw the sheets all messed up on the floor and started to fold them again."

"And then what happened?" cries Suzanne.

"Shh," says Rachel, slurping her tea, more interested now.

Pam leans back with her mug, takes a sip, glancing at each of them in turn.

"Then I heard a sort of growling, then a chattering sound. A clicky sound. Like someone grumbling, muttering in another language. I couldn't make out words. The laundry muffles everything. But it was strange. I didn't like it much at all."

Beryl and Shirley look at one another.

"I don't like it at all, either," says Beryl, and shivers.

"So then I said, 'Hello? Who's there, then? Are you lost?'" And for a moment or two, there was complete silence. Nothing. Then I moved forwards and *fwump* again, only this time it was me, knocking over some shirts. Then I heard a crash. I went over, heart thumping, and called out, 'Who's there? What do you want?' And there was a screech and a muttering. It sounded close. I didn't like it at all. Then I saw a flash of something. It leapt above me, knocking the washing again. I saw a bit of reddish fur and a shadow above me, like a man swinging on the ceiling. Then a great heap of stuff came down on top of me, and I couldn't see anything after that."

"Why didn't you tell me about all this?" says Marie, whose brow is creased and eyes wide.

"I don't know," says Pam, a slight smile at the edge of her lips. "It only happened on Wednesday. I tidied it all that night. No harm came of it."

"But if the person is dangerous, or needs help?"

"Well, I've worked it out, and having thought about it, it's not a person at all."

"Oh!" says Beryl, her pale skin turning paler.

"Not a ghost, Beryl, don't be daft. It's not as if anyone has died here. No. An orangutan. That's what it was. I'm sure of it."

Rachel coughs up a short laugh.

"A what?" She glances at Nerissa for a moment, and then back to her grandmother. "How do you figure that?"

"It's obvious to me. Once I thought about it. Nothing was taken, so it wasn't a thief. It didn't try to attack me. Nobody answered when I called out, because they didn't understand. And the sounds it made weren't human. But it was too big to be a cat—it had arms. Then it jumped and swung in a way a man never could. And the red fur."

"You're a regular detective, Nan."

"You might mock me, but how else do you explain it? Since Nerissa is here, I thought I'd ask her what she thinks."

Nerissa is sideswiped by the story. She has just begun to believe there is a stowaway aboard, so widespread does the rumour seem. But she had not considered the possibility of an orang. She wonders if it could be Molloy, somehow, but his proportions, his shape, his abilities, are too different. Her thoughts scan through the animal deck, trying to decide what it might be. Everyone is watching her, waiting for an expert opinion.

"Um. It's hard to say. The reddish fur, the ability to swing. That could indicate—"

"See! So I said."

"But I wouldn't necessarily expect it to run away. It's not from our deck, either; we didn't bring any orangs with us. So if it was, it must have stowed away when we set off. I don't see how. And it would be hungry, looking for food. Others would have seen it."

"We don't know they haven't," says Beryl.

Nobody speaks for a moment. There is a falling, fluttering sensation in Nerissa's stomach. She feels spooked, like Beryl, as if she has heard a ghost story.

"Should we report this?" says Marie. "It could be someone in danger. Somebody sick—all those strange sounds. If it is an animal, it needs to be found."

"I'm adamant it's an ape of some description," says Pam, unfazed by the experience but determined to be believed.

Orangutans

Nerissa remembers the orangutans up close, when she worked with them in Sabangau National Park. She was told there were only 4,000 orangs left in the world. Sabangau was somewhere to preserve this creature and to hone her skills. At first, she hated it: the cloying, close rainforest heat leaving a permanent sheen of sweat on her skin. Leeches clamped to her ankles. The odd, rotten smell of the durian fruit, heavy and spiked and clustered on trees wherever she looked. Chairil, who lived and worked permanently in the park, introduced her to the orangs. Those, she fell in love with, and she resolved to stay for four months because of them. She loved their coarse, russet fur and their dark, tree-bark skin. She loved their long arms and soulful eyes. She had never encountered creatures like them. They were solitary for the most part, keeping away from one another except if they wanted to mate, or if they were very young. Groups of juveniles would tumble about with one another in the foliage, or on the decks built against the trees. The older males had big, floppy cheek-flaps like rubbery plates, with shadowy, deep-set eyes.

Nerissa watched them each day and made notes in her logbook. She crouched down, or climbed to a platform in the trees. Chairil would harness her up, smiling broadly, and come back in an hour to help her down. She had never liked heights and would sit close to the trunk of the tree, her legs trembling. But she would stay and watch and soon become absorbed. She saw one young female, nicknamed Dusty, create a little pad of leaves to hold the spiky durian fruit, lipping out the creamy insides without hurting her fingers. The same female made a canopy of leaves in the rain. Chairil took Nerissa to the river one day and gave a young male a bar of soap. The orang stood in the green water, soaping up his leg.

"See, he's clever," said Chairil. "He knows how to wash."

The orang looked at them both and then bit gleefully into the soap.

"Well, he's getting there."

Nerissa listed their food: *wild figs, cracked eggs, honey (which comes with risks), insects.* She tried some of these foods herself, Chairil choosing the best insects for her. Once she had stopped thinking about their eyes, they were okay. He told her about the bush-meat trade and the illegal logging that had finally stopped. He said that palm oil was a problem. Everyone wanted it. And it was right there, in the park.

"There are rules, but the government doesn't always win in these things. Sometimes small groups come. Sometimes they bring violence."

He told her the orangutans would be extinct in twenty years. He was here to help them, but he was still certain it was futile.

Chairil was small, a little shorter than Nerissa, with nut-brown skin, his face lined despite his young age. His torso was stocky and strong. He laughed easily. He read her short poems he'd written, which he knew she didn't understand. Then he translated them and laughed as if it were all a joke. She wondered how much was lost in translation, but he seemed to write about the rain; cloud leopards (which she'd never heard of); bats living in long, dark caves; sleep; dreaming, and food. In his own language, he part-spoke, part-sang the lines. In English he spoke and chuckled. She suspected he was deeply intelligent, but could not communicate that side of himself to her. But instead of being frustrated, this seemed only to make him happy.

She slept in a bamboo-framed hut with coconut fibres for a roof. The huts were spaced far apart. She sometimes heard footsteps, soft on the ground outside, but she was left alone. She was not the only Westerner. There was a small group of researchers or journalists who had arrived a few weeks after her. She had kept to herself and the villagers she knew, and somehow had still not got around to speaking to them. Not being well understood had its attractions.

One night, the villagers put on a puppet play: a traditional *wayang golek*. Chairil talked her through the narrative. It seemed to go on for hours, with eating, talking, and laughing coming from everywhere. Many of the jokes were dirty, some of the lines beautiful, and the puppets moved elegantly around the stage. She went back to her tent around 1:00 a.m., the shadows of puppets still moving on her eyelids.

She woke from a light sleep and heard breathing in the pitch-dark, deep and moist amid the tinkering shrill of insects. She touched her fingertips lightly on the mosquito net, but did not move. Someone entered and whispered a word she did not know. She recognised his shadow: Chairil, pulling back the netting. She wasn't afraid or even surprised. He rested his body lightly over hers, then gradually his whole weight. Up close, his skin smelt of smoke and rain. He lifted her T-shirt and moved her legs apart. She put her hands on the small of his back, all the time looking him in the eyes. It was as if they'd never met.

The next day, she went to a deeper part of the forest, feeling prickly with humidity and bugs. She was resting on the ground, propped against an elegant teak, when a voice came from above.

"Hello down there. I don't think we've met."

She tipped her head back and scanned the canopy. Thirty feet up, a young man hung on a harness, camera slung across his shoulder. He looked as though he had slipped and was twisting precariously on the rope. Nerissa looked around for someone else who would normally be there, making sure the rope was anchored.

"Are you okay?"

"Sure." He laughed, resting the toe of his boot against the trunk.

"Do you need help getting down?"

"That might be nice."

Nerissa wasn't that good with ropes, but she remembered how Chairil set them up, and looked carefully at the anchor in the ground. After a few minutes, she figured out how to roll the slack in and out, and hoist the climber down. He got greater purchase near the bottom and half-climbed the last ten feet or so. When he reached the bottom she saw him closely, sweat beading on his curved upper lip. He smiled like a character from an old movie and began unclipping his harness.

"I'm Greg. Silver." He put out a damp, warm palm.

"Nerissa Crane. Where's your partner?"

He looked around him for a moment. "My … ? Oh, I came here alone. I usually do. Are you working here?"

"Yes. I'm a trainee vet. I'm learning about the orangs."

"Me too. I mean, I'm taking photos of them. I work for *National Environment*. And a bit of freelance stuff."

He lifted his camera. His eyes were grey-blue, his hair dark, cut in a long crop and tipped with droplets from the canopy. He was lean and broad-shouldered, with a looseness in the way he held himself, as if he didn't know how to worry. He was twenty-five, though at the time Nerissa guessed him slightly older. While she spoke to him, she could still feel the echo of Chairil's body slipping gently inside her.

Nerissa walked back with Greg, glad of being with someone sure of the way. Everything in the forest seemed to duplicate itself, and sometimes it took her longer than it should to find the village again. He picked a spiky durian fruit as they walked.

"I still can't eat those things. They stink," she said.

"Well, they do say, 'smells like hell, tastes like heaven' … or something."

He split it open, and the ripe, rotten scent gave way to the creamy fruit nestled inside. He scooped a section out.

"Just try, go on."

She wrinkled her nose, but nibbled the edge. It was smooth and tasted to her like a mixture of cheese, tobacco, and vanilla. Greg told her about photographing the orangs and other creatures too. The Bowerbirds, eccentrically decorating their delicate nests to attract their mates with gleaming bugs, flowers, mushrooms, even the wrapper from Greg's lunch.

"I had to rescue that. They liked the shiny bit. They go to some trouble for their lady friends. Some of my mates don't even clean their bedroom before a date!"

They left the project at Sabangau not long after. She wanted to stay, but the area became dangerous. Government rule was crumbling, and palm-oil prospectors became more desperate, trying to come into the reserve. A boat was arranged for the small group of Westerners. The day they left, there was a thunderstorm, and she couldn't hear what Chairil was saying as she said goodbye, hugging him like an old friend in the rain. He smiled and chuckled, as he always did.

They travelled upriver, Nerissa quiet with her notebook. At night, they burned candles on the deck to light their way. The rain went on for days as their boat slipped along the river. They sat under the tarpaulin draped over the deck, Nerissa with her notes, Greg clicking through his images, taking apart and cleaning his lenses. The small group took turns heating tins of soup or trying to wash their few clothes in the muddy river. People talked in low voices about their research and the families waiting for them.

The first night the rain was a silver curtain. They looked out at the densely covered banks, hearing the sound of distant gunshots. Or perhaps it was thunder, or old trees cracking and dropping to the forest floor. They didn't speak about it. Nerissa thought of her night with Chairil and how out of character it had been of her. She felt as though it had happened to someone else.

On the third evening she sat next to Greg. He showed her photos from the trip. He had captured the orangs perfectly—they trusted his lens. He'd reach his fingers out before him as he crouched down to them, and they would sometimes reach back. Or they would swing above him, scattering rain and bugs from the canopy, sending the bright birds up.

On the fourth night she sat next to him again.

"What will you do after this?"

He looked up from wiping a lens and took a slurp from the mug beside him. "Find another assignment. I keep thinking about underwater creatures. Or maybe something political—you know, hang out with some activists."

"Is there much point in that now?" said Nerissa, gazing out at the flat, black surface of the water.

"Ah, so, a pessimist? Why the orangs, then?" He looked intently at her, as if willing her to lift her head higher.

"I think there's a point in learning as much as possible, but not in protesting. It's better to prepare."

He snorted then, but rather than feel insulted, Nerissa smiled, pleased to be goading him.

"Action is what's needed. It's never too late."

"Some things are."

They paused then to see a crocodile raise its crooked shadow from the water. Greg raised his lens, without camera attached, as if he might shoot it.

"There used to be these creatures called river dolphins," said Nerissa. "They were white. Or sometimes pinkish. They looked like ghosts. Friendly ghosts."

"That croc didn't look friendly," Greg said laughing.

Nerissa smiled again. "A river dolphin hasn't been seen since the beginning of the century."

"So, they really are ghosts."

"Yes."

Greg dropped his voice, and lightly touched her arm. "If I ever see one, Nerissa, I'll take a photo and bring it to you."

She looked away, embarrassed, and said, "Would you do anything for a photo?"

"If it really mattered that the world sees something, I might risk my life. I'm not a war photographer, but I might take a calculated risk. Maybe."

A thrill ran up her arm then, where his fingertips still lightly rested.

"You don't get scared?"

"No. I'd climb up something, swim under something, go somewhere I shouldn't, if a good shot were waiting. Why be scared? What's the worst thing that could happen that won't happen someday anyway?"

She picked up his coffee cup, with its thin trail of steam, and sipped from it without asking. It was late; the forest and the river were dark as tar, and they slipped through in their shadow boat, the silent captain steering them, his face impassive, and the sound of the low murmurs of the others around them. Greg smiled.

"I get scared," Nerissa said. "Heights especially. And deep water. Even when I know I'm safe, it's my body that doesn't think I am. It's like I have thousands of pairs of tiny wings under my skin, all on fire, trying to fly me out of there."

Greg laughed. "Well, that's odd. But I think I know what you mean. You know what that feeling really is, though?"

She looked up at him, but saw no change in his expression of amusement.

"It's the feeling of being alive. And that can only be good."

He leaned towards her, and she thought he might kiss her. She could see the hazel flecks in his irises and the stubble on his cheek. But he reached behind her instead, into the water, and touched his damp hand to her hot cheek.

So this was how they met. Before the water came. Before she worked for the Institute. Everyone in the village is almost certainly dead now. When she returned home, she was told that her father had died. She tried to imagine when. When she was with Chairil that night? When she was watching the strange puppets? When she was noting what the orangs ate or did on a particular day? When she saw Greg, suspended from the tree in the green light? She did not feel it happen, did not register the loss as she thought she should, even at that distance. Why didn't something give way inside her? Why didn't her breath stop or a feeling of dread overcome her? It seemed unforgivable that she had just carried on living.

Molloy

squeezes through the hole he's made, dust from the wood catching in his fur. Here there is grass, long and glossy, parting as he moves, and soft, black earth damp on his paws. A carrot-flower, white and floaty, bobs into the camera, brushing the lens. He tugs at it, chews, pulls against its root. There are cabbages, sweet and stinking, nestled in rows. He snuffles into them, heavy and clumsy, crunching down on their blowsy leaves. He scrabbles into the soil, releasing swarms of bugs and the slick bodies of worms. He wolfs down their meaty selves. Then the ground vibrates and a shadow moves across him. He looks up, sees a woman's face. There is something covering her mouth. Her long, gloved fingers disturb him. At the last moment, Molloy dashes away, back through the hole of his own making. The men are still there. Something long and metallic clatters to the ground. Up the vent he goes again, sure of a threat, the earth still clumped around his whiskers. At least he is no longer hungry. He hears voices below him, fading as he makes his way up and up.

"I don't know. It looked like a dog or something."

The pipe widens, its edges squaring off. It turns from metal to thick wood. He stops here, peering through a gap. He can see feet, very close. The camera records the detail of the shoes: polished to a shine and fastened with buckles. The floor beyond is pale and shiny. Farther off, a group of people stand with their backs to him. The recorder picks up their voices, faintly, but clearly enough to transmit what is said; a device sending images and sounds nowhere for no one to see or hear.

"This runs automatically, I believe," says one. "So we don't tamper with that. There are some things here we can change."

She is leaning over something that protrudes from the wall of the room, and gesturing with her fingers. Then she takes it, pulling it down towards her like a lever.

"What about the Doubeks in Deck Eight?"

"Yes, of course, they keep things ticking over. General maintenance. They report to me if anything happens. But nothing should."

Molloy looks up, shifting the camera to an abstract angle. A porthole swings into view, a dark shape cutting across it.

"So, if I do this, and this, that ought to take it—"

"Are you sure? I would take it like this, using this one, make it steadier."

"I see, yes."

There are two women reaching over each other, their arms working at the lever, twisting it and pulling.

Inside Molloy's small stomach, something drops away, making him dip his head and draw in his paws. He has forgotten what he was so eagerly pursuing. And he has forgotten the way home.

Diving

She and Greg were never able to agree on what their first date had been. He insisted it was when they got off the plane in London and he asked her to go for a drink with him in the airport bar. She had been tired, sipping on a rum and coke, turning the straw around and thinking of the village. When she recalls it now, she realises there was a glow in Greg's cheeks, his eyes fixed on her, bright in the grey light. He drank his beer like water and bought another when she'd still barely touched her drink. As they left he leaned in for a hug, and there was a slight tremble in his shoulders. An hour later her taxi joined the push of traffic heading into the city, and she watched the clouds piling up in the sky. There was bad news waiting for her.

They didn't speak again for some time; she was caught up in funeral arrangements, in selling her father's house. As far as she was concerned their first date was the scuba-diving lesson. They'd both moved closer to the coast by then, her for work, into a small bedsit, him into a shared house to get out of the city, so he could "breathe". She had concentrated on her work at the little clinic, on the care of people's beloved pets. She had tried not to think about anything else. He called her, saying he'd always wanted to be able to dive so he could photograph sea life.

"Isn't the Channel a bit grubby? I mean, would you be able to see anything?" She felt a prickle of sweat over her skin as she spoke, knowing he was asking her out. She paced her flat with the phone tucked into her neck, smiling. Could he hear the smile in her voice?

"Well, I'm hoping for something more exotic once I've got the licence. Anyway, the first lesson is in St Leonard's pool."

"Very exotic. So, no danger of sharks, then?"

"Ha. Well, you never know."

She sat down, shifting the phone to the other ear.

"I'm kinda scared of the water."

"Scared of heights, scared of the water? Anything you don't have a phobia about?"

"Mmm."

"What better way to overcome it? Think of the coral reefs and the beautiful fish you might see."

"All right," she said, a flush rising into her cheeks. He made her feel as if she might do anything.

The pool echoed with their voices, the light rippling in streaks across the walls. She was self-conscious in her bathing suit and didn't know where to put her hands. Greg was more handsome than she remembered, hair slightly longer and sticking up, lean-bodied, with wide shoulders and deep T-shirt tan lines, a slight softness in the belly. He had hairy knees. He was grinning. She still had a long plait then, which she could feel tickling at her bare back.

Once in the water, they were taught how to breathe through the regulator; to use buoyancy control to rise and sink; to signal to one another. Nerissa slipped under the water and found that she could breathe. She saw Greg and the others, turquoise on the pool's bottom. Sounds softened and whooshed around her ears. She could take out the mouthpiece and put it back without panic. Water was a strange new peace. She was exhilarated afterwards. They went for a burger and chips and grinned at one another from red, plastic chairs that were bolted to the ground. Greg chomped down on his burger.

"You've got a lovely bum in your swimsuit," he said.

She laughed. Somehow, coming from him, this comment was okay. Later, on her doorstep, they had kissed, the taste of relish and ketchup in their mouths. She closed the door on his smiling face.

After the second lesson, she invited him in. They didn't think of eating. Her hair was still damp, and the skin at his shoulder tasted of chlorine. He joined his hands around her back and lifted her up towards him.

Whales

Nerissa sat on the beach in Santa Barbara early in the bright morning, the back of her wet suit still unzipped. She checked her diving computer, her regulator and her yellow "octopus"—the backup—three times. The water looked steely, with waves crackling onto the shore. Huge pelicans drifted on the air currents and then suddenly dived down, as if drilling into the blue skin of the world. Greg came along the beach, carrying the tanks.

"Come on, Riss. Rob says the boat's ready."

She stood, and he zipped up her wet suit, giving her a quick kiss behind the ear. He was flushed with excitement, and once in the boat, he frowned over the casing on his camera, making sure it was watertight. Rob skippered their boat. He had a broad, swimmer's body, stretched ear-piercings that looked like plugs, and matted hair with a greenish tinge from all his time in the water. Nerissa thought of him as a kind of contemporary, non-criminal pirate. She'd never seen him wear a shirt.

"We've got a good chance of seeing them today," he said. "There's a female or two in heat."

It was Greg's dream to catch a heat-run, where a group of males chase and jostle to win a female. On that first day, it wouldn't happen. But they saw the female and her calf. Rob juddered the boat to a halt and let it drift, seeing a dark shape, like a coral reef, darkening the sea about ten metres away.

The creature emerged slowly, like a submarine, the water gushing down her back. Her skin looked like tree bark or ancient rock, striated and ridged. Green-edged barnacles decorated her all over. It was as though she'd been carved from a cliff and set into the sea. Her body turned sideways in the water, drawing alongside their little fishing boat, which dipped and bobbed in response. Nerissa looked into the whale's intelligent, old eye. It puffed a geyser of water at them from its blowhole. Nerissa held her breath, not sure if she had ever seen anything so beautiful.

"Completely awesome!" breathed Rob. Greg was at the edge of the boat, pulling his flippers on. He'd told Nerissa over breakfast that a whale's heart was the size of a car, and that its tail fin had the span of a light aircraft's wings. It turned in the water again and began to descend. Nerissa stood, mesmerised.

"Come on, Riss!"

She sorted her kit out, Rob helping her to strap the tank on, and joined Greg in the water. The female had gone to rest on the seabed, but as Rob entered the water, her calf powered up to him. He seemed to want to play, and as Greg trod water, rolling his flippers out then back, and taking photos, the young whale swam past him, his powerful tail whooshing inches from Greg's body. Nerissa kept more distance; she had not been so far from land before with only the dark green of the sea stretched out around her. Her legs tingled at the thought of the deep water. The mother hulked like a shipwreck some feet below.

"That was amazing!" said Greg, as they hauled themselves back into the boat. "He was playing like a puppy."

"You want to be careful," said Rob, his teeth flashing. "One snap of that tail, even from the small one, and *bam!*"

Nerissa unhooked herself from the gear, wondering how the word "small" could apply to something as big as the boat she was sitting in. They had not seen the males yet, come to battle it out for the female, but they had a week to go. Greg gave her a salty kiss, and the boat turned to take them back.

They ate salmon salad and chips that night, sharing a bottle of wine, and walked along the seafront. She'd dressed up, lining her eyes with dark brown kohl, staining her lips with 'briar rose'.

Her face was wind-blushed and twinkling with powder. She wasn't sure if Greg noticed. The sea was invisible beyond the sand, but announced its huge presence with a rush and drag. Back at the motel, the beige sheets were scratchy and the bed small. Greg stretched out on his back and fell into a deep sleep. She lay awake, tears smarting in her eyes. He had never ignored her like this. His only thought was for the whales, for the pictures. His eyes seemed to glaze, and he spoke of nothing else. She wondered why she was there with him, if not just as some kind of witness to an adventure he starred in.

On their final day of photographing, what Greg hoped for happened. They watched the female and her calf, who by now were used to their presence. The early sun was un-sticking itself from the horizon. Rob called out, "Here they come!" and they saw great shadows in the distance. The males were speeding towards them. One heaved out of the water and turned, sending shockwaves towards their boat. The female took off, steaming away from them, five males in pursuit.

"We have to get in front," shouted Greg. It was their only chance of capturing any shots. The fishing boat powered on beside the heat-run, engine thrumming. Nerissa watched the water at the very edge skimming away. Greg had been diving without his oxygen tank for a few days, so as not to disturb the whales. He came up for air every few shots. He decided it was best to do the same now. They stopped the boat and he dived in, waiting for the group to pass above him. Despite her feelings, she was excited for him, excited for herself as these creatures surged through the water for one purpose that nothing could stop. She imagined the images he could take from amongst them. Nerissa watched Greg's head bobbing on a wave, and then he disappeared as the female approached. They came like attack ships, males crashing into one another, the tiny boat shuddering in their wake. They were huge and beautiful: landmasses suddenly animated. She could not see Greg. One tail fin, coming slightly too close, could knock him unconscious.

The shadows rushed on. She counted. Thirty seconds had gone by, at least. She glanced at Rob, but he stared straight ahead, eyes narrow, hands at the boat's wheel. A minute. Maybe more. The water foamed and eddied where the whales had passed. A minute and a half. Two more bullied along, and the boat tipped down hard, then bobbed back up again. She sat down and gripped the rail. Two minutes. Surely it was two. She watched for Greg's head, trying to see his shadow beneath the surface. But there were bubbles and mini whirlpools shattering the sea. More than two minutes now. She couldn't count, feeling her seconds must be too fast or too slow.

"Rob," she said, scrambling for her gear. He turned to her, and before he could say anything, there was a long gasp from the water.

"My God!" Greg was holding the camera above him like a trophy. "That was incredible!" He flopped over onto the boat, rivulets trickling from his hair and pooling at his feet.

"Greg," said Nerissa, thumping his chest, her open palm meeting the weird texture of his wet suit, "you were down there for ages."

"I know. I was just about to come up, but then one just swam above me. I had to get it."

Rob draped his arm around Greg's shoulders. "That was awesome," he said, grinning. "Let me get us a beer, man."

He popped the bottles open on the deck and handed one to each of them. Nerissa joined them in clinking the bottles together, but then sat alone as they chugged back, draping her hand in the water, tears smarting in her throat again. She wanted to shout at him, ask him why he'd risk his life, why he'd be willing to leave her on the boat with Rob, searching for his drowned corpse all evening. But she couldn't bear to in front of Rob. She could hear Greg, still breathless, saying, "Then she took her mate down, down to the bottom. You know, we still don't know what happens down there; no one's ever seen it."

"I'm going to sit on the beach a while," she said when they got back. She walked down the pier before he could reply. She knew he was paying Rob, and saying farewell, so she waited, watching the pelicans, her peeled-off wet suit in a grey heap beside her like a shed skin. She saw Greg approach in the distance, his wet suit rolled down to expose his torso, an extra pair of slack arms dangling at his waist. She stood, ready for a fight about how she'd been rude, ready with her words about his selfishness. She took a long breath so her voice would be steady. But he looked at her and reached down to catch her hand. Not smiling: his poker face. His nose was sun-caught and peeling, and a bloom of freckles spread over his cheeks. She noticed a slight tremble in his fingertips. He knelt down in the sand.

"Nerissa, marry me?"

Letting Go

"Okay, so I've decided to go."

Herman looks up from his broom, the indigo, submarine light bisecting his face. A zebra, mostly in shadow, blasts out an impatient breath.

"Where?"

"To the Letting Go Ceremony. Are you going tonight?"

"I'll come, yes, if you prefer not to go alone."

"I don't mind. I'm just going to hang back. See what's what." Nerissa is suspicious of the ritual and afraid of her emotions, but her curiosity is greater than these feelings.

"So, what do I need to know?"

Herman brushes down his overalls and walks towards the hatch. "Well, I'll just change. Don't really want to take this animal shit with me. They do it in a corner of the school deck, in the biggest schoolroom, after the kids have gone. Last time, people had pictures, you know, of loved ones. Everything else was already there. The pictures helped, but you didn't have to. I might take one with me tonight. A wedding photo, maybe."

"I'm just going to watch."

"Okay. Sounds good. You might want to ..."

She narrows her eyes, and he thinks better of saying any more about the ritual. Instead, as they leave, he turns to her and grins. "I didn't say, I like the new haircut."

She runs her hand through it.

"Thanks. It's made me feel a bit more human."

There are others there when they arrive. Perhaps thirty of them. The light is low. The steward, Tabitha, stands at the front of the schoolroom. Her expression is calm. She is dressed more glamorously than usual, in a long blue skirt. She is not wearing her utility belt. Another steward, with beautiful ebony skin, stands beside her. People line up to receive a small, lit candle. On the floor of the room there are neat rows of wooden bowls filled with water. The water reflects the orange light of the candles and the children's artwork pinned around the walls. Nerissa stays at the back of the room; she does not join the queue. Tabitha notices her and nods. Herman touches her elbow and quietly joins the others. Nerissa sees several people she knows amongst them: Nick, the chef; Marie and Gus; the women from the laundry, all collecting their lit candle and seating themselves in front of a bowl. Everyone looks dressed up, as if for a party. None acknowledge her. Each is intent only on their candle and their bowl. As they sit, some produce a photo and contemplate it, waiting for the others to settle. Some carefully roll up their sleeves. Finally, they are all seated. Marie and Gus hold hands. They have two images of a child between them.

"Welcome," says Tabitha, "this is the Letting Go. You are all aboard the *Baleen* because you are special. Because you have been chosen. Because, together, we will create a new and better world."

Then the ebony-skinned steward speaks. Her voice is different, like a metallic song, and it makes Nerissa feel chill and strange.

"Much of the land is lost. Many of our loved ones are lost. You will make a new society on new land, out of the chaos. You have been chosen. Do not hold onto those you have lost. Do not grip them tightly. Let them go."

There is a silence, during which the *Baleen* seems to hum, and Nerissa imagines she hears the muffled press of the water against the hull. The candles flicker. She sees faces darkly reflected in the bowls of water.

"Take your picture of your loved one if you have it, or hold their image in your mind, and repeat our words," says Tabitha. She and the beautiful steward begin to chant a low, haunting song that could be coming from the ship itself.

"Do not hold onto me."

"*Do not hold onto me,*" the group repeats, murmuring, their eyes half-closed.

"I am only a memory."

"*I am only a memory.*"

"Let me go, so you may live."

"*Let me go, so you may live.*"

Their voices rise in intensity. The words reverberate around the curved walls of the schoolroom. Nerissa feels them in her ribcage and deep in her belly.

"I will not hold onto you."

"*I will not hold onto you.*"

"You are only a memory."

"*You are only a memory.*"

"I let you go, so you may live."

"*I let you go, so you may live.*"

"I let you go, so we may live."

"*I let you go, so we may live.*"

In the stark silence, Nerissa's stomach lurches. She feels nausea rising into her throat.

"Now," says Tabitha, "take your photo, your image of your loved one, and cast it into the ocean. The love of the ocean will take them."

Each person with a photo takes it and dips it into their bowl, immersing it in the water. Those without a picture plunge their hands in up to the wrists. They smile as they do so, as if released from something. Nerissa sees the photographs, distorted by the water, the faces of people that are not here, not on the *Baleen*. She cannot imagine how anyone could have left another behind. Those pictures must all be of the dead. Those precious photographs. It is as if they are being drowned all over again. She rushes from the schoolroom, bile rising in her throat, tears blurring her vision.

Wedding

They had joked about getting married in a lighthouse.

"You'd never get everyone to climb all those stairs. Think of your Aunt Elaine in her stilettos," said Greg.

"All the decorations would have to be round. Pom-poms. Glitter balls. It would be cool; you can't deny it."

As it was, they had married in Old Brighton registry office, the blue carpet damp, the walls cracked, both in their Wellingtons. It was just them and two neighbours as witnesses. Greg wore a cord jacket and a gold bow tie. She was in short, vintage lace with a bouquet of sunflowers. Afterwards, they took the open-top bus up to the Birling Gap, high on a bottle of cheap pink fizz, the coastal roads twisting away. He lifted her up when they got off the bus. Her hair had tangled in the wind. He almost dropped her, then they raced to the edge of the cliff, where they saw the Seven Sisters and the way the green land rose and dipped away from them, and then, in front of them, it just ended. Greg wrapped his arms around her waist and kissed her neck.

"It's crazy," he said. "Now we're together forever."

"It is a bit crazy. And brilliant. You and me. No stopping us. Hitched."

They both stared out, feeling the land beneath their feet holding them up. The wind was cool and strong on their faces, whipping their best clothes around their legs. The ocean was dark green and stretched out before them, as far as anyone could see.

The Mithras Institute

National Environment had asked Greg to photograph a shipwreck.

"It's just a couple of weeks, Riss."

"I don't like the idea of it. It seems dangerous. And what if they move us on again?"

He was packing a bag on the bed, avoiding eye contact. He always did that when he was hiding something.

"We're on the third floor, so why would they? And it's dry as a bone out there," he said.

She flipped open the blind and looked at the street. It was strewn with roots and old bottles, sodden paper, faded and ripped clothes. Anything could wash up anywhere. Nerissa had lost her job, the local animal clinic finally forced to close after being left without proper equipment, the electricity failing. They had been married two years, moving from communal bunk-barns to crumbling flats. Money was low.

"Why won't you just stay?"

"Because I'm going crazy. This is good money. We need the money. The salvage part is lucrative, but the pictures will be amazing too. I have a duty, don't I? So people don't forget about these things? What's not to like about this?"

"So I'll come with you."

He looked up then. "No, no, I don't think you should."

"So you are saying it's dangerous?"

"I'm not saying that. Why do you try to catch me out all the time? It's a rough job. Horrible digs, dirty lifting, you know. It's trickier. It's a bit of a man's world out there. I don't want them to give you a hard time. Or me, to be honest."

"Is it illegal? Is that it?"

She was close to tears. For weeks he'd been distant, bored, smiling thinly at her, avoiding her touch at night. "I'm just exhausted," he'd say. She didn't really want to go on the dive; she was testing him. Maybe he could tell.

"It's not illegal. It's with *National Environment*. You're so uptight."

"Just shut up," she said, throwing a ball of socks at him that she knew he needed to pack. "You're a selfish shit, that's what. You need to grow up."

He sat down on the edge of the bed, fiddling with the straps on his bag, and scowled at her.

"Trouble with you," he said, "is that you do everything they say: 'It's going to flood, you're all gonna die, give up your nice flat, your decent job, go from pillar to post with a sleeping bag and two bog rolls. It'll be a great bonding experience for everyone …' "

"In case you hadn't noticed," she shouted, "our home *was* flooded, our stuff *is* trashed, and we can't go back there because it's underwater."

"Sure. But now, now this is just paranoia. I'm going to live my life. I'd rather drown than die of ennui."

"I'd rather you would too."

He laughed then, pleased with her anger, as if it was the most fun he'd had in a while. He caught her arm and drew her over to the bed.

"Come here," he said, his voice low. "We can't go on like this. We're practically prisoners. I'll go, I'll get us some money, quick money, and we'll start again. Luxury bog roll! A better place. Things' ll change."

She saw him off at the port, fearing she would never see him again. In the weeks that followed she dreamt of him drowned, suspended in the ocean, his eyes marble-white, his hair streaming into the water. She'd wake in a sweat just before dawn and walk the streets, tasting salt in the air, watching people moving their few belongings into boarded-up houses. While she waited, she tried to have normal days that weren't too long. She woke as late as possible, getting up when the sun was breaking through the grey sky. She went out for supplies from the half-empty supermarket, dragging big bottles of water and tins of syrupy fruit back to the flat. She combed the beach for things of use—plastic containers, pieces of glass, anything they might need. Faces peered from broken windows. There were empty cafes, their chairs and tables waiting as if for customers, but their counters and kitchens were blown out and salted. There was nothing to do here but survive. In the evenings she read until the light faded, the same books over and over. Books were so heavy they had left them behind as they went. After the novels, she went back to her textbooks and traced the anatomies of creatures drawn beautifully in their old pages. As soon as it was dark, she slept.

One morning, returning from her walk after the sun had wobbled into the sky, she heard someone crying out, "Nerissa, Nerissa", their voice muffled by the wind, "Ms Crane?" The voice caught up with her. A teenage boy with ruddy cheeks and a tuft of dark hair. He was breathless.

"A letter," he said. "It's for you."

She took it from him. The wind threatened to snatch it from them both and send it out to sea. She clung to it. She couldn't speak. She smiled thinly instead, looking at the boy as if he was a member of her family, a child all grown up that she hadn't seen for years. But he was a stranger, like everyone else. She climbed the stairs, frantically pushing her fingernails into the envelope, and sat down on the bed with the door to their flat still open.

May 7th, 2095
Corsica
Dear Rissa,

I've no idea when you'll get this – post seems a bit slow here, but it is getting out. I'll keep trying to call, but the queue for the phones is ridiculous. We've been busy out at the wreck. You know what I'm like. But I'm thinking of you and I miss you. You're my babe – I love your bones. You know that.

I wanted to write and tell you about the wreck. It's awesome – beautiful. I'm glad I came, despite the terrible food and my damp bunk! I share with Stanley, a wiry old seaman if ever I saw one; like something out of a book. He's got some of his own stories to tell too. I'll save them for when I see you. He passes this rum around every night that knocks your socks off!

But the wreck! It's stunning. I've enclosed 3 shots I managed to print. I wish you could see it. It's like a cathedral – a green cathedral covered in weeds with big blocks of light filtering down. There are layers to it – corridors to swim through and rooms. Jewellery still in drawers and a bath tub you can pretend you're taking a bath in. We've prised off a couple of lobsters to compensate for our bad dinners. We've taken some amazing pictures. There are little jellyfish like UFOs. And fish that change colour – matching the metal and wood in the ship. Wreck-diving is where it's at, Riss. It's like going into a haunted house; you half expect to see a spook.

I know I've been here too long. There are delays with the boats, God knows why. No sign of anything untoward. No sudden floods like at home. And home's been okay too, I hope? I'm keeping an ear on the news. I'm back in two weeks, the 21st, by 3:00 p.m. See you on the dock. And let's not fight any more…

Love and a big kiss,

G. xx

She took the photos and lay them down on the table one by one like tarot cards.

The first was of the top part of the wreck, carpeted in weeds and glistening with clams, a wedge of golden light shining down into the water.

In the second, boxes of crockery and silverware, glimmering a purplish blue, were set on the bottom of a coral-encrusted stairway. The only clue this was not a grand house was a fellow diver hovering above the stairs.

The third photo was the boat from above the waterline, its dark shadow hulking greenly beneath them like a sea monster. There was gentle turquoise water all around. Greg was off to the right of the image, grinning, his mask pulled away from his eyes, his eyes narrowed and shining in the sunlight. A shot taken for her.

He was coming back soon. It was always Greg who had the adventures. He would have things to tell her; he'd be flushed with new memories. While she waited, she tried her best to tidy the flat. She washed down the windows with soapy water and went through her college books, arranging them in alphabetical order. She sat on the creaky bed and leafed through *Veterinary Anatomy*, reading her own pencilled notes in the margins. Near the back, slipped into a page on the anatomy of rats, she found a yellowed business card with a stylised image of a bull on the front and an address and telephone number in Istanbul on the back. The Mithras Institute. She remembered the glamorous redhead at her graduation, her offer. It was probably too late; the Institute may not even exist anymore. But it was worth a try. She pulled on her boots and left to use the communal telephone. The voice that answered was both familiar and strange. She thought of those red lips, pursed around the glowing cigarette.

"Ms. Crane. I had hoped you might call me one day."

May 12th, 2095
New Brighton
Dear Greg,

I'm so excited to see you when you come back. I've missed you. Your photos from the wreck are beautiful. I hope you have not been too hungry and you don't smell too bad... You know I love you, and I'm sorry we fought.

I've got something to tell you: I've been offered a job. A real one. A good one. It's good money, they said we can both go, and we get a flat. It's in Istanbul. I think things will be better there. We'll talk when I see you. Big kisses,

Yours always, Rissa. xx

She took the letter to the post office, apprehensive about Greg's reaction. He could be angry at the thought of being moved again. But they were accomplishing nothing here.

The day she met him at the port was fine, the sky a benign blue, grey clouds mackereling away to the East, letting the hazy sun dry the damp jetty. He came off the boat with his bag slung over his shoulder, a swagger in his walk. His hair was salt-coarsened and his face tanned. She wrapped her arms around his neck.

"You smell of seaweed."

"I love you too."

She drew back, looking into his face.

"So, what did you think about my letter?" she said.

"I think it's brilliant, Riss." He took her hand and hoisted the bag farther up his shoulder. They walked along the jetty. "I've already made some enquiries. There's a *National Environment* office there. They have a few assignments for me to do. Let's do it; let's go."

He gripped her hand more tightly, and turned his face to her as they walked. She was so pleased, she could only grin.

The call to prayer came out over the city like a sad song, an ululation as Nerissa and Greg woke each morning in the near-dark. The Institute gave them a flat with high ceilings, five stories up, looking out over the semi-submerged old town and the bulk of the Hagia Sofia in its biscuit-coloured light. Greg even made a darkroom in the utility, since there was no washing machine or fridge in there anymore.

"I love to develop the old-fashioned way. Use the old Pentax sometimes. There's nothing like watching the images form, like magic, from nothing."

Over the decades, the waters of the Sea of Marmara and the Bosphorus had crept higher, controlled by the flood defences at Galata Bridge. But it meant the old town, from the domes of Hagia Sofia—now neither church nor mosque—to the university, could only be traversed by boat. This lent great charm to this part of the city. Where car horns had once blared from the gridlocked streets and then trams had scythed around its ancient buildings, only gondolas, canoes, and small motorboats slipped quietly through its passageways now.

Each morning, Nerissa took a taxi-boat from the front steps of their building to the offices of the Mithras Institute, which were built over the Basilica Cistern. The Byzantine reservoir, from the sixth century, was the purest water supply in the city, and the Institute used it for their experimental work. Esther Mortimer had given them a tour. She looked the same as she had when Nerissa met her at graduation, her bobbed red hair perhaps a little longer. Her heels clicked on the walkway.

"Have you ever seen anything like this?" she said to Greg, touching his arm. His eyes were wide in the dim light. The water was waist-deep below the walkway, and the great columns holding up the structure seemed to recede into infinity. It was a watery, disappearing underground palace, sonorously dripping and lit with an amber glow. Old coins shimmered beneath the surface, huge fish moved languorously, as if made of gold. Esther's soft voice echoed back from the shadows.

"I'm so glad you could join Nerissa here," she said. "I would love you to photograph this part of the facility, for *National Environment*. It's a stunning piece of history, don't you think? And still being put to good use."

"Really. I could? I'd love that. I'll see what they say at work."

"Of course." She touched his elbow, leading them deeper into what locals called *yerebatan sarayi*: the sunken palace.

"I want to show you both something."

They turned right along the walkway, the gorgeous, glowing pillars seeming to multiply beside them and behind them.

Drips echoed into the water and occasionally anointed their heads and shoulders. Nerissa leant over the rail, and a droplet rippled her reflection on the dark surface. The air grew damper, and the shadows took on a greenish hue as they turned left, into the far corner.

"You know the story of Medusa?" said Esther, turning to face them and pausing in her stride. "The gorgon who could turn a man to stone with the serpents she had for hair?"

"Of course," said Nerissa. Greg nodded, looping his arm around Nerissa's waist.

Esther, beckoning them to follow, headed down the metal steps. A huge stone head, set upside-down, supported a great stone column. A smile played on its grey lips. Its eyes were calm. Medusa, hidden in a shadowy corner, her skin slippery with dampness. And Medusa again, another one, with a similar face and those carved coils of serpent hair, placed on her side, supporting another column.

"Pagan fragments. Protectors of temples for the Romans. These heads probably belonged to bodies once and stood guard on a monument or a tomb. No one is sure why they were put here. Or why they are upside-down."

Nerissa wondered if it was to reverse or diminish Medusa's petrifying power; bring those turned to stone back to life.

"Some say, they were simply the right size for the columns; it was just necessity. Others that they wanted to imprison her here, so to speak, to never see daylight again. We pump the water from this section, so they can still be admired." Esther headed back up the stairs, as Nerissa and Greg lingered to look at those impassive, enigmatic faces. Greg leaned down, turning his head to see their faces right-side up, to read their expressions. Esther stood with her hands resting lightly on the railing.

"Personally," she said, "I think our ancestors liked keeping those two ladies down here, to visit them from time to time. To know their power was still around."

The offices of the Mithras Institute were light and airy, well-designed and equipped. When Nerissa first arrived in Istanbul, she'd been startled by the structures around her: high-rises with extra rooms built precariously on them, their concrete exposed; derelict wooden houses, rotten in the damp, encrusted with lichen and barnacles, being reclaimed by the sea; mosques like huge shells. While Greg could not stop taking photos, it had unsettled her. But when she stepped from the taxi boat into the pale lobby of the Institute, a sense of calm surrounded her.

Above the reception desk, there was an ancient stone carving protected by a sheet of glass. She studied it whilst the receptionist called Esther. It depicted a figure emerging from a rock with a flowing robe, then again, wrestling a bull, twisting it into submission by its horns whilst driving a spear into its flank. Animals were carved into the frame: a crow, an eagle, a lion. A lobster and a dolphin curled in the bottom left. A dog, a snake, and a scorpion, coming up from the bottom of the image, seemed to drink the bull's blood. The figure turned back to a bright, shining sun.

"This is very old," said Esther, appearing beside her, "even older than the cistern."

On that first day of work, she'd sat in Esther's office on a grey velvet sofa, and Esther had poured her apple tea into a tiny glass cup. Nerissa balanced the saucer on her palm, finding nowhere to set it down. Esther had walked around the room at first as she spoke, pausing occasionally at the bookcase as if to check certain volumes were still there.

"I'm pleased to have you here, Nerissa."

"Thank you. I'm pleased to be here."

"You seem so grown up now."

Nerissa blushed, shifting the saucer into her other hand. The tea was still too hot to drink.

"You seemed young at your graduation. Now you're married. You've gone through some difficult times." Esther gazed out of the long window with its view of the top of the Galata Tower. The call to prayer began, the imams answering one another in song over the city, echoing through loud speakers. Esther talked over them, as if she couldn't hear it. Nerissa was not used to the prayer's stark beauty, punctuating each day, slicing through the moment.

"It's not been easy for anyone," she said.

"We've done irreversible damage, that's for certain," sighed Esther. "Us, our parents. And so on. We all know it. There have been so many floods, dating back as far as we have records. Think of Gilgamesh, or the flood in Ovid's *Metamorphoses,* or Noah. What happened to Atlantis? Probably a flood in what used to be Santorini, and that's gone too now. The tsunami in the early part of the century, before you and I were born. The earth does this from time to time, doesn't it?"

Nerissa only nodded, thinking of her old home.

"But the rains seem to be subsiding," said Esther. "Perhaps we can manage, with defences ..." She trailed off and took a long gulp of tea. Nerissa touched her own cup to her lips, but found it still scalding hot.

"What I'm concerned with, Nerissa, are animals. They are so important to the ecosystem. Even ugly ones." She laughed, a warm grin spreading across her features. Then she sat in the armchair opposite Nerissa, placing her cup and saucer on the floor. Nerissa did the same.

"So, Mithras. It is my inspiration. I like the drama of the thing. Historians know little about the cult and can only guess with their few fragments of manuscript and wonderful carvings like the one I acquired for the lobby."

"So, it's about a sun god?" asked Nerissa.

"Well, not exactly, and yes, in a way. Mithras is born from a rock and related to Sol in some way, part of him, or on the same team. He wrestles the bull, and various creatures take its blood. The religion had certain grades and people became initiates through trials, re-enactments. We don't know what they involved, exactly." She sipped her tea again, and Nerissa found hers had finally cooled enough to drink.

"My own interpretation is not about showing strength by killing the bull, but about wanting to harness its spirit, as it were, for all the other creatures. So that was my inspiration for the name of the Institute. That and my love of those artefacts. The one in the lobby is from the third century."

"Wow," said Nerissa. "I can barely wrap my head around that date."

"Wonderful, isn't it? Let me show you the lab."

The lab wasn't clinical and white as Nerissa expected, but furnished with warm wood and steel worktops. One section had two sinks and deep cupboards, machines and equipment tucked into purpose-built alcoves. The other section housed live animals: rabbits, mice, rats, snakes, some small birds. There were tanks containing miniature turtles, eels, and bright fish. The enclosures were large, and a hatch could be opened during the day for the small mammals to graze in a little garden. Their bedding smelt fresh, like cut hay. It was partly her job to maintain this standard of care. She was to work with Angus, who was younger than her, dressed in a black linen apron, with a flamboyant moustache that he curled up at the ends with wax.

"Hey," he said, extending a gloved hand. "Great to have you on board."

As they left the lab, Esther told her in a low voice, "Angus graduated two years after you. Top of the class. But your grades were higher."

On her first working day in the lab, Nerissa turned up to find it pitch-dark.

"Angus?" she called, feeling around the unfamiliar walls for a light switch. "Angus?"

The lab was silent. Then, in the far corner of the room, she saw a green glow. The glow began to move with a strange lolloping gait. Another luminous ball joined it. There was a fuzzy quality to these odd moving blobs of light. Suddenly, one seemed to float up before her, coming closer, levitating towards her face. She stepped back in alarm, bumping into the worktop. As the glowing bundle grew close, she saw its bright eyes and almost translucent ears glowing even more luminously than its fur. Then Angus's face, his black moustache, his shining eyes, illuminated in green.

"Wooo," he said softly, and the lights came on.

He was holding a small, white rabbit, and there were several others padding around the lab. He laughed.

"Glow-in-the-dark rabbits. Never seen one? Everyone wants one." He slapped her on the back and pressed the warm bundle into her hands.

"Come on, let's put these critters back, and I'll take you for coffee."

Angus had his own shabby canoe with an outboard motor. They puttered through the streets to his favourite floating coffee house in the Grand Bazaar. The little boat chugged up Tavuk Pazari, past the dome of the Nuruosmaniye Mosque and through the stone archway with its crossed flags and gold Arabic script above its title: *Kapaliçarşi*. Inside, the blue and red paint remained on the archways of the ceiling, the plaster patchy and crumbling. The walls were lined with floating market stalls. Boats weaved around each other, and shoppers and merchants called out, haggling for the best price. A man floated past in a tiny boat, barely more than a raft, its motor spitting. He carried trays of tea-glasses, sugar cubes and spoons, his wares shining like lanterns. Blocks of spices, coloured deep red, ochre, purple, and green bobbed gently on their stalls. The scents of saffron, mint, and cloves mingled in the damp air. Merchants leant out precariously, toes on the edges of their jetties, asking them to touch silks and taste dried figs. The market echoed with chatter.

Angus moored his canoe at a coffee shop, and she took his hand, unbalanced on the floating platform. She was glad to settle at a table. She felt the floor move slightly when one of the larger boats went past.

"Sorry," Angus said, "I'm a bit of a joker. I always do that to newbies." He ordered two Turkish coffees, and they came in blue and gold cups.

"Teşekkür ederim," he said to the waiter. He plopped a sugar cube into his cup.

"Transgenic bunnies," said Nerissa. "I've never seen one in the flesh. Are you using jellyfish DNA?"

"Yes, but I really want to find something that glows pink. For my girlfriend. Just for fun. Esther doesn't mind the odd personal project."

Nerissa sipped the thick, rich coffee. "Which technique do you use?"

"Sometimes microinjection into the cell. I'm experimenting with retroviral and transposable, looking for better rates of success. Anything that means they pass on the alteration."

Nerissa remembered first learning about transgenesis on her degree. She liked the complicated stuff. There was a memorable lecture from Professor Hughes on Freckles, the spider-goat. Hughes commanded the lecture hall with his strong Yorkshire accent and his square jaw.

"It was a great breakthrough," he said, flashing an image of an ordinary-looking goat onto the projector. Freckles was white with a brown patch on her nose. She had a lopsided mouth and a dopey expression. The students had giggled.

"This was just in the second decade of our century, and this little lady was a bit special, despite appearances. The gene that encodes dragline silk, from the orb-weaver spider, was put into her DNA, the part that tells the udders to make milk. And voila, a goat whose milk contains strands of silk. This could be extracted for all kinds of uses. It is so strong; it's perfect for repairing ligaments. In today's lecture, I will tell you how they did it."

They had scribbled everything into their notebooks, determined to understand the procedure. The exam for this class was notoriously tough. But Nerissa loved lessons on DNA. She understood it as a language that was common to everything. More universal than music or maths. Since all cells used this language, none were truly foreign to each other.

Angus drained his coffee. "I've got lots of ideas," he said. "Ways to make animals more resilient. To withstand hot sun, go longer without food or water. Horses with completely waterproof fur, like duck feathers. Flying cats …"

She laughed. "Better get back to work, then, Angus. Show me what you have already."

Months passed at the Institute, happy, productive ones. She and Angus were just a small part of it; she often wondered what happened in the other labs and longed to find out, when she was trained well enough. Nerissa sometimes felt uneasy at the few failed experiments, but otherwise, the work was satisfying. It made a change to make animals stronger, adapting them to avoid extinction. It was better than treating them when they were sick and their lives already failing. But with rodents and fish and frogs, all safe in the lab, she could hardly imagine their trials crossing into reality. She would think of the orangutans often, of how she might still make them able to survive the violence of the disappearing forest. A solution like that seemed beyond her grasp.

Greg spent his time documenting the vast city for *National Environment*. He was out all day, sometimes on the other side of the bridge, beyond Galata Tower. He'd go to where it was still possible to walk dry streets, taking the tram to Taksim Square to drink with, and photograph, local radicals. In the evening he worked in the darkroom and would invite Nerissa in to see shots developing in the trays of liquid, illuminated by red light. There were dynamic images of whirling dervishes: monks in their shroud-like robes, with tombstone-shaped hats, captured mid-spin, turning with the universe. He had images of the Blue Mosque, which could be entered only by elegant longboat, its thousands of azure and white tiles as airy as the sky. Sometimes he would kiss her in the red-dark. "We can't leave," he'd say, "not till the photos are fixed. Let's think of something to do while we wait."

The three of them, Greg, Nerissa, and Angus would go out into town after work. Greg never left his camera behind. Angus put them in his canoe, which dipped down at the back so it was only just above the water. They smoked apple-flavoured tobacco through beautiful glass *nargile* pipes, bobbing on damp seats in the warm back-alleys. Smoking was illegal except in particular cafes, and the floating tables were always packed. But Angus knew everyone, and they could always get served. He told them life was less fun before they arrived, as Nerissa got lightheaded on the sweet smoke.

On weekends they hitched on ferries going out into the sea, watching rolling waves of mist curling down onto the water and burning away in the sun. They ate blue fish and red fish in old restaurants with peeling facades and were often the only customers. Angus's girlfriend was round-faced and fearful of the large boats and open water, and preferred to take Nerissa into the cramped, floating bazaars to haggle over silk scarves and bright spices. Everything in Istanbul was alive, chattering with sound, moving through water. Shadows and ribbons of light rippled against the walls. She thought often of the shipwrecked look of her old home, the drained skies and the sand sifting into abandoned buildings. In Istanbul, her heart was beating like the hearts of the animals she worked on: quick, nervous, and warm.

One Sunday, Nerissa woke from a dream that she was slipping from the bed. She sat up with a start. There was a note on her pillow.

Dear N. Looked like you needed a lie in. Gone to photograph Cistern. Esther said today was a good day. Back soon. Will bring baklava! Gxxx

It was late. She saw the hazy sun over the city, big-bellied clouds weirdly illuminated from beneath. There was a commotion outside, and as the sleep cleared, she heard sirens. Not unusual in itself, but there seemed to be so many of them. She looked out of the window to the sand-coloured bulk of the Hagia Sofia to her right. She caught sight of their tiny kitchen through its doorway as she turned. The floor was littered with smashed crockery, and the cupboards hung open. She turned to the other window and looked out towards the Mithras Institute. She couldn't see its rooftop. Fast ambulance boats were cutting through the water on Yerebatan, creating waves that rocked the smaller boats trying to get out of the way. People were shouting. People were screaming.

A tremor, caused by a grumbling shift in the earth, had created a wave. The wave had crashed through the ancient pipes and flooded the Cistern, niggling into a hidden weakness in one of the pillars. And then they had all gone as the water suddenly rose up: pillars falling into pillars in a great stone catastrophe, bringing the Institute and its years of research down with it. It was a Sunday, and only a few people were at work. Angus was one, working on a pink glow-in-the-dark mouse for his girlfriend. Greg was another, photographing the Cistern. When Esther told Nerissa, her face was grey as granite, her hand shaky, gripping the stub of a cigarette.

"The waters rose too quickly for anyone … ," she said, not looking at Nerissa, "Then the pillars fell. And then everything was buried. The entire thing."

Nerissa was numb. She went back to the flat that evening. She could think of nothing to do but stand in the red light of the darkroom, printing one of Greg's images from a random roll of film. She cannot remember what it was. It is as if she never looked at it. She just recalls her hands, plunging into the cool developing fluid, red all around her, dark shapes blooming on the paper.

Electrical Storm

Nerissa confronts a kind of ghost: rimmed with silver and suspended against a green-black background. This is the first time she has thought to look. What she sees seems as alien and familiar as a dream. It is dome-headed, the layers of its being both transparent and obscure, curled in on itself. The details are illuminated, then recede as she rolls the transducer around. Its heartbeat flickers like lightning in the distance. She hears a soft intake of breath behind her.

"Nerissa?"

Herman stands there, a tray of sandwiches balancing on his big palms, his red eyebrows high on his forehead.

"I was going to tell you, Herm. I guess I was just getting used to the idea."

He walks in slowly, placing the tray on the examination table and peering at the monitor. Nerissa has the transducer resting against her belly. He looks at her face.

"How long have you known?"

"Since before I came aboard. Just before."

She drops the transducer, and the screen turns dark with a flicker of static. Herman sits down, lifts one of the sandwiches, then puts it back down on the plate.

"I thought there was something. I just couldn't put my finger on it."

Nerissa sits too, perched on the worktop next to the sink. She takes a big bite from her sandwich. Neither speaks for a while. Herman turns his sleeves down and buttons them. Eventually, he eats a sandwich, chewing slowly. Nerissa tidies up some implements, putting them into jars and compartments.

"My wife left me," says Herman to the back of her head. She turns to him and leans against the worktop.

"It was about four years ago now. We didn't have any kids. We just kept putting it off. I got complacent; I had no idea she wasn't happy. But I think life became boring for her."

"Do you think that was the reason?"

"I wasn't much fun, grumbling all the time about cleaning graffiti from the corridors. She found someone else. We kept in touch—you know, Christmas cards. Sometimes a letter. I got the sense from her letters that she found the floods thrilling at first."

Nerissa nods as Herman talks, offering him a slight smile.

"I would have taken her back in a second. I'm not sure if she knew that."

"Do you know what happened to her?"

"I do. But only because it was on the news. There was footage. I shouldn't have even looked at it, but I thought I recognised her among the faces. And then I wanted to be sure. It was the debris in the water. It moves faster than you think. The waves themselves are more powerful than you think. From a distance, you wonder why they can't swim out. They look so surprised about it."

Herman and Nerissa sit for a while.

"You could have told me, Nerissa. I would make sure you get enough food. I always would."

"I know, Herm. I'm sorry."

"Don't you think you should see the Doc? I saw him—he's all right, I reckon."

Before she can answer, the dark monitor comes to life with a bright flicker, and here is the first officer's face, her black, almond-shaped eyes reflecting a porthole, the glimmer of a smile on her red lips. They turn to watch.

"Good afternoon to everyone aboard. I trust you are well and settling in. The stewards report on your excellent work and peaceful cooperation. We are impressed. I am addressing you today to inform you that we are in the process of fully submerging the *Baleen*. You may notice this when you look through the portholes on Decks Five and Six. This is nothing to be alarmed about and is merely a precaution."

She clears her throat and smiles broadly.

"We have detected a possible electrical storm, and this manoeuvre will keep us out of harm's way. You will not notice any changes in the *Baleen's* movements and, indeed, we are taking this action to ensure comfort and the normal running of the vessel. Should you have any questions, please ask your nearest steward. Keep up the good work."

A smile again, and the screen flickers into darkness. The message has dispelled the intensity of their conversation, and neither can think of anything to say for a moment. Nerissa stands from her slouch against the worktop.

"Should we do anything?" asks Herman.

"I'm not sure there is anything to do. Let's just wait and see."

"Okay. And thanks. You know, for listening to me."

Nerissa smiles. "I'm going to rest for a while. If you need me, just knock."

She squeezes his shoulder as she passes by.

Darshana

When she wakes, Nerissa goes to the porthole and pulls back the cloth. She cannot feel the descent of the *Baleen,* but the sea looks darker; it has taken on a purplish hue. There is a fluttering, dragging feeling in her stomach. She imagines the storm, black, thick, flickering with pale lightning above them. And then there is a flash of silver at the corner of her vision, far out: a light in the deep shadow of the water. She closes her eyes for seconds longer than a blink and opens them. There, pulsating in the shape of a globe: a shoal of metallic fish. Mackerel, she thinks. Turning, blinking their dark eyes, rolling past her window. Alive.

There is a knock on the door.

"Come in," she says. Her voice comes out as a whisper.

Herman stands on the threshold. She turns back to the porthole. It is dark and blank again.

"You okay?" He gives her a quizzical look.

"Yeah. It's just … I thought I saw something out there."

"Maybe you did." He looks agitated, half turning his body from the room.

"Maybe. What's up?"

"Darshana Hardy, the first officer, she's here. In your workroom."

"Great, at last someone to speak to."

Herman offers a half-smile. "She doesn't look all that happy."

"Oh, okay. Don't worry. I'll speak to her."

Darshana Hardy is slim, small, with dusky skin, and liquid black eyes like a deer. As they enter, she's looking at Nerissa's instruments, running her finger along the work surfaces.

"Nerissa Crane?" She puts out a reedy hand.

"Good to meet you."

Darshana sits in the one chair and draws out a tablet, scrolling through it for a moment, then looking up. Herman stands behind Nerissa, twisting the ring on his left middle finger.

"Herm, can you make us something? Chicory coffee?"

He nods. "I don't have any sugar at the moment."

"No problem," says Darshana, giving a tight-lipped smile.

Nerissa leans against the examination table, lifting the weight from her back.

"I'm glad you've come, Officer Hardy. I had a few things to ask."

"Okay. Well, why don't you start?"

"I had wanted to ask how long we might be at sea. Some of the animals, they don't do well confined for too long. In close proximity. You know some have died already."

Darshana looks down at the tablet. As she tips it in the light, Nerissa notices a long crack on its screen, carefully mended with transparent tape.

"An African elephant. Two llamas. One gecko. Seven Syrian hamsters. Fifteen canaries …"

"Yes. I reported them all. And causes of death, if I knew."

Darshana puts the tablet on her lap. "I understand the difficulties of your job, Ms Crane. The captain wants to make sure we find an appropriate place to land. So we do not have to do this all over again. We have predicted eight months to a year at sea. We've only been here a fraction of that time. There are unpredictable factors, such as these storms."

"It seems a long time."

"Yes. But also short, given the circumstances. Do you need us to help you more? Are there certain supplies, or facilities?"

"No, the Garden Deck does a great job. It's working pretty well so far."

Darshana stands, clipping the tablet to her belt.

"I have another question," says Nerissa.

The first officer turns up her palm.

"I just wondered why all of the stewards I've seen are women."

"Ah, yes. That was a conscious decision. We felt that female authority figures would prove less threatening, given the history. It is sexist, of course. But it seems to work. Now, I want to take a look at the animals."

"Sure. This way."

They descend to Deck Twelve via the ladder. Darshana seems nervous climbing the rungs, tentative and weak-armed for someone in her position. She holds a square of cloth over her nose as they walk among the animals. Nerissa tells her about each of them: their ages, habits, diet, as well as where each originally came from. She stops by Reva, the Indian elephant, and offers her a half-peeled banana. Reva's trunk rolls out and Darshana shrinks away.

"Reva is gestating. The calf seems good. There are some months to go, but I suppose she'll probably have it on board."

Blue light from the portholes filters in, illuminating motes of hay-dust and shining on Reva's deep-set eyes. Darshana types something into the tablet.

They ascend into the workroom, where Herman is waiting with coffee. Or something very like coffee. Darshana sips hers eagerly.

"Herman does so much of the work," says Nerissa. "Feeding. Mucking out."

Darshana glances at him.

"I have to ask you both about something. There have been reports of an escaped animal."

Herman flashes Nerissa a look.

"Not the orangutan?" Nerissa says.

Darshana frowns, looks down to her tablet. Herman stares at Nerissa and silently mouths, *What?*

"You don't have an orangutan on your inventory. No, no, it wasn't one of those. I'm confused."

"Oh, it was just a daft story I heard. Probably a joke." Nerissa flushes. Why has she said anything?

"No, it was described as a dog, or a wolf or a fox. The report came from Antoinette, in the Garden Deck. Yesterday."

"There are only a few dogs aboard, but we don't have them. Families keep them as pets."

"Yes, but we've checked, and none are missing."

"How can you be sure? If one went missing, even for a short while ... And there's a big difference between a wolf and a fox."

Darshana scrolls through the inventory on her tablet.

"We have checked. And people don't know that wolves and foxes are so different, if they haven't ever seen a real one. Do you have any missing animals? That is the point."

There is silence as she scrolls. Nerissa glances at Herman, who avoids her gaze and shifts his feet around on the floor. Too late, he's going to say it.

"All right. It's my fault. Molloy. The Woolly Rat. He's missing."

Nerissa puts her hand to her forehead and sighs.

"Yes, I see this rat on the list. It was not downstairs. But surely a rat would be smaller?"

"No. He's a rainforest rat. Not like a common rat. He's really big. And woolly."

"How long has he been missing?" Darshana says sharply. She is really looking at Herman now, as if she has just noticed him. A red blotch is deepening on his neck.

"Not that long."

Darshana looks at each of them in turn. "You realise this is serious. Rats aboard a ship, spreading disease. Eating supplies."

"He's not that kind of rat," says Nerissa. "He's very docile. Almost tame. He's rare—the last of his kind."

"I don't see what you mean. He's a rat. A rat is a rat."

"Not at all."

Darshana folds her arms. "Regardless, the not-so-tame rat will be destroyed if a steward comes across it. We can't have rats on the loose. Frankly, I'm surprised this wasn't reported immediately."

"Please don't kill him," says Herman, his face collapsed and stricken.

"Look," says Nerissa, "we need his DNA, to preserve his species. In case there aren't any more of them. If you kill it, then … "

"I will report this to the captain, and ask the stewards to be vigilant. If you want your rat alive, you'll have to recover it yourselves. If a steward finds it … "

"But why are we keeping all these animals, if not to save them?"

"That's one thing. A rat loose on the ship is another."

Social

The next afternoon, Nerissa goes to find Herman. He is with the animals. It is becoming darker as the *Baleen* descends, and she takes a torch, its beam picking out hundreds of wary eyes. Herman emerges from the stables.

"Aren't you resting? I'm fine with the feeding."

"I'm not an invalid. I just came to tell you I'm off to have a look around."

"What will you do?" He wipes the dark sweat from his neck with a handkerchief, and shifts the sack on his arm.

"I haven't looked hard enough for him. I'm going to go out, be methodical about it."

"I should do that. It's my fault we lost him."

"No. He escaped. And who can blame him?"

Herman looks down and runs his hand across his brow. "Will they kill him if they find him first?"

"That's an empty threat. Don't worry about it. They wouldn't. If they actually saw him." She isn't sure of this. She thinks of him, sitting beside her as she reads her books, the light on his camera flashing, his little nude mouth working on a morsel she's fed him. She remembers the soft, scruffy feel of his fur, the heat of his body, the pulse of his working heart against her palm. For a moment she conjures an image of him dead, the light gone from his polished eyes, his body stiff.

"Not everyone likes woolly rats," says Herman.

"Oh, I don't know."

Herman fiddles with the catch on the chinchilla enclosure. Its occupants turn their heads to the sound like worried, giant mice.

"Is he already dead, do you think?"

"Oh no. Don't say that, Herm. I think he's probably stealing food, making a nuisance of himself. That's why he's not back here yet. Not hungry enough. Look, I don't want you to worry about me. I might take a while to find him. I'll pop back here for sleep. But we might miss each other, be a bit ships-in-the-night."

"But I ought to go," he says again. There is a deep wrinkle between his eyes.

"You have to look after all this for me. I'm a bit of an invalid, remember?"

His face softens into a grin. "All right, but remember to eat." He presses two of his own brown tokens into her palm. She doesn't refuse them. She leans forwards, rests her hand on his shoulder, and gives him a quick kiss on the cheek.

Nerissa starts on Deck Five, where she sees Gus again.

"You look great," he says. "Check out the hair. Très chic, n'est-ce pas?"

"If you're testing my language skills, you won't get far. But thanks. Marie did a good job."

"So, what's new in the animal world?"

"Not much. Still smells of manure. It's getting darker down there. I don't think it suits them well. We have lots of artificial light; we're keeping it on longer. Lots of energy."

"Nothing to be done."

"No."

Deck Five, where the edge of the ocean can usually be seen through the portholes, is totally immersed. The water shivers against the glass.

"I have branched out today; the Mender helped fix the plug on the waffle iron. You want one?"

"Not today. I'm going to go to Social."

Gus turns down the corners of his mouth, leans onto his elbows. "For socialising?"

"Something like that."

Social's expanse of decking is set out before her, with the steely canteen along its edge, various tables and benches set out. She looks at Greg's watch. It's nearing seven now, so the place is busy with people queuing for food, families calling to their children, who are chasing around. A group of people play an intense game of mahjong at a round table flanked by circular stools. Some teenagers are working on papier-mâché masks, pressing strips of damp paper over moulds. All she can hear are voices, overlapping, clamouring. A few people look up as she makes her way between them to the queue. Some smile. She catches the edges of conversations as she goes, meaning rising up through the white noise.

... "I thought he was cute, but, I don't know, if it didn't go well, he'd be hard to avoid"... "I'll swap you three brown tokens for two red"... "I am old enough—how am I going to get lost here, anyway?" ... "always the cabbage. Cabbage stinks"...

Nerissa selects a vegetable stew and some dense, dark bread. Then she glimpses who she's hoping for, his white-blond hair poking out of a headscarf.

"Nick."

He frowns at her. "Do I ... ?"

"Not really. Gus introduced us, but—"

"Ah, yes. The quiet one. Good choice of stew. I made that. Hope you like it, bit spicy."

"I'm sure I will." She breathes in the warm steam. Nick's eyes are dark and intense. His lopsided mouth could be smiling; it's hard to be sure.

"I was wondering, could I come back there, see how you do all this? I'm curious."

"You've aspirations to be a chef? Am I right?"

She looks down, allowing herself a chuckle.

"Oh, I don't know. I'm just interested in what happens behind the scenes, I guess."

"I don't normally, but there's something about you I like. I liked it when we first met. You're a listener." There is a definite grin here now. "Come on, you eat while I chop."

Behind the counter, in the kitchen, it's hot. There are eight people at wooden blocks, stirring great vats, or pummelling dough. They all wear salvaged aprons: multi-coloured, striped, spotted, even one with a comedic naked torso. Nick chops onions while she eats.

"We run a tight ship, so to speak. I get a bit frustrated because we don't have much to work with. I was professional before. Had my own fish restaurant. Not much fish here. Ironic, huh?"

He attacks the onion. She smiles through her food, gulping it quickly. It burns in her throat.

"We must supply the odd thing," she says. "Prawns."

"Even a bit of meat a month or two ago, when a few things keeled over. We had some good rabbit stew. Some snake. We told people that was beef. It's better than beef, I reckon."

"So where do you store all this?"

"Over there, big cupboard, or the refrigerator boxes."

Another onion fragments under the long blade. There are little nicks and scratches all over his knuckles. His skin is scaly and hard, as if it has healed over many times.

"Can I see?"

"It's not interesting, but go ahead. It's not locked while we're here."

She slides off her feet and pulls back the heavy wooden door. Nick has his back to her in the kitchen, chopping and sifting. Inside are rows of shelves and big sacks of what looks like rice and wheat. There's a subtle tang of mould and over-ripe fruit, warm earth and cheese. She looks quickly and carefully on every shelf, shifting packets, blocks of dry noodles, cartons, some battered tins. She tries to see behind each shadow. She draws out a pencil torch. No signs of gnawing or nibbling. There is one vent at the back of a shelf, with a metal grille. She peers into it.

"You all right?"

She jumps.

"Oh, you scared me. Sorry. Of course, yes."

Nick steps into the room, wiping his fingers on his apron, drawing the door in with him until it is almost closed.

"Listen," he says softly, "if you want extra food for yourself ... Whatever you want it for, you only have to ask. Some people, it's the food they miss most. Not the amount of it; we're not starving anyone here. No, it's all the different flavours. The scents. The textures."

He reaches up to the highest shelf and brings down a small, orange jar. He opens the lid, approaches her, and holds it close to her face.

"Here, smell it."

She inhales, her heart tapping against her breastbone, looking beyond his bulk to the door. Chocolate powder. Buttery, dark. A hint of vanilla and tobacco. She thinks again of the durian fruit. Of Greg asking her to taste it. Nick puts a hand onto her waist, places the jar on a low shelf, and draws his other arm around her. She feels his breath at her neck, hot and paprika-scented. His sweat smells feral.

"We all have something we miss. I'm happy to trade—"

She pulls away, plucking his fingertips from her. A feeling for her baby rises into her chest.

"Take your hands off me—don't touch me. You misunderstand me. I haven't come to take anything. I only wondered."

For a moment, she thinks he'll close the door on them. But his eyes clear and he steps back.

"Sorry," he says. "I'm a bit of an idiot. Sorry. I just get—"

"It's all right. I've got to go now, though. Thanks. Thanks for letting me see where you work. All the stuff."

He opens the door, and she steps into the fluorescent light of the kitchen. Everyone is busy, haloed by steam, pulling trays from ovens. There is a huge tray of mashed potatoes topped with cheese, being sliced into squares. She thinks of school. As she walks around the front, back into Social, the air cools. Nick hands her the orange jar.

"Nick, I don't need—"

"Have it, though."

She wants to believe he's given it to her out of kindness. In her room, unable to sleep, she dilutes half a teaspoon of it into hot water and milk. Tomorrow she will go to the Garden Deck, where she knows Molloy has been seen. The baby pushes a foot or hand against her belly, touching the inside of her skin.

Molloy

scuttles through the darkness of the pipe, licking condensation where he comes across it, his pink feet slipping and splaying on the metal. He hears voices again and smells the sweet, milky, sweaty scent of young people, mingled with something strange and spicy, which curls in lines of smoke coming up through a grate. The camera bumps against the steely sides of the pipe, and Molloy pauses over the mesh of the grate, looking down into the schoolroom. He doesn't know that he has circled back here, drawn by the pheromones of youngsters. It is nighttime, and if Molloy understood human time, he might wonder what this group of teenagers are doing here. Wisps of blue smoke from burning incense reach him through the mesh. He breathes the odd, cloying scent and becomes tired, resting his head on his paws, looking sleepily below him.

Each teenager wears an animal mask made of papier-mâché and painted in bright colours. They each hold something bright and steely in their hands, and stand in a row in front of water-filled bowls. They face two adults. One of these wears an intricate, wooden lion mask, painted ochre with a stylised muzzle picked out in black ink. Her red hair is combed neatly behind her ears. Her lips are shiny and red. The other wears a shimmering china crow's mask with a curved blue beak. There is a box beside them, covered with a cloth. The woman in the lion mask is speaking to the teenagers, her teeth starkly white in the darkened schoolroom. Molloy's device picks up her voice.

"Welcome, Initiates. I am excited you are here."

They face her silently, some with slight smiles.

"You have been preparing for this ceremony your whole lives, in a way. Learning how to use your gifts. As you pass into the next phase of your lives and your bodies mature, some of these gifts will deepen. And new gifts will emerge."

The woman with the crow's mask speaks. Her voice is thinner, almost shrill.

"You will repeat our words, and then complete your first task."

The teenagers shuffle slightly, and Molloy hears them draw in a collective breath. One adjusts his dog mask. Now both women begin to chant, lion and crow, their voices rising in song.

"Like the whale, we can traverse the ocean."

The teenagers join them, their voices uncertain at first, some mumbling.

"Like the whale, we can traverse the ocean."

"Like the camel, we can survive the desert."

"Like the camel, we can survive the desert."

"Like the bat, we can navigate the night."

"Like the bat, we can navigate the night."

Their voices rise, becoming confident, taking on a rhythm.

"Like the lion, we are fearless."

"Like the lion, we are fearless."

Some voices are cracking in their excitement; some are coming out as sobs. The metal pipe vibrates with sound, and Molloy draws away, his camera capturing a lop-sided view of the grate, losing focus on the figures below.

"I am stronger than the bull," the women cry.

"I am stronger than the bull," return the youngsters.

"I take on the spirit of the bull."

"I take on the spirit of the bull."

"I am all creatures."

"I am all creatures."

There is a silence. Molloy shuffles back to the grate and peers down. The crow-faced woman draws the cloth away from the box. Inside, tiny creatures chatter and stir.

"Come up," she says, "and take one for your sacrifice."

Molloy turns, spooked by the smell that comes from the box; a naked, pungent smell. He speeds into the darkness of the pipe, his paws sliding on its cold interior.

The Climb

According to Darshana Hardy, Antoinette from Deck Three, the Garden Deck, had been the last to see Molloy. Apart from the food cupboard, or the few places where waste food might be missed, this seems like the only other attractive place. Nerissa knows he's been scared away from there, that no one was able to catch him, but perhaps he has found a way to hide. She knows he will return to where he can find food. The long grass and moist earth might remind him of home. At the very least, she can speak to the person who saw him last. She can't help the feeling she is barely missing him, going to places he has been recently, or is about to arrive at as she leaves.

She wakes early, though the purplish light tells her nothing about the time. She dresses in thick leggings, a shirt, and a tank top. Her workroom is quiet and still, slightly chilly. On a scrap of paper, Herman has written: *fresh apples in the filing cabinet*. She hauls the drawer open and takes two out, one for now, one for her small rucksack. The apples are the palest green and look unreal. She takes a bite; the flesh is dry but aromatic and sweet. She adds thick gloves and a cloth bag to her rucksack, along with two pencil torches, the jar of chocolate, and a small glass bottle of water. She is tired and lightheaded, wanting only to sit down and close her eyes.

When she gets to the lift, a red light is flashing. An electronic message ticker-tapes where the floor numbers usually show: ... LIFTS CANNOT BE USED WHILE THE BALEEN DESCENDS. PLEASE TAKE THE STAIRS FOR DECKS UP TO 5. DECKS BEYOND 5 CANNOT BE VISITED TODAY...

Today, of all days, when Nerissa wants to visit Deck Three. She climbs the wooden stairs to Deck Five; the rails are lit by tiny LEDs that pinprick the gloom. Deck Five is still quiet. Only a few vendors are setting up their stalls. Gus is not around; the plastic awning of his stall hangs over a cold and empty hot plate. A steward with teak-brown skin and long, jet-black hair is sitting on a barrel, drinking from a steaming cup. She smiles and beckons Nerissa over.

"You're pregnant, aren't you?" she says simply, her voice musical and deep.

Nerissa draws a barrel up next to her and perches on it. "You're the first person to notice."

The steward sips from her mug. "Or the first person to say so. Is it four months, five?"

Nerissa nods.

"You're skinny, but you can tell by the way a woman holds herself, more than anything."

There is silence. They both watch the dark water on the portholes. Nerissa thinks she catches movement beyond them.

"Look after it. It may be the first born aboard. It is special."

A baby born between lands, with nothing solid beneath it.

"Can I ask you something?" says Nerissa.

The woman nods, the tips of her hair skimming the decking.

"When the lifts don't work, can we take the stairs?"

The steward looks surprised, as if expecting some profound question about motherhood.

"Yes."

"But they go no higher than here?"

"That's just because we didn't get the stairs finished in time. We need to get working on that. It's a pain for the few working on the Garden Deck. But they can stay where they are for now. They have their own food. Laundry will be closed today. But I'm sure it won't last long. The lifts will be recalibrated. Or the storm will die down and we'll go back up."

She sips from her mug.

"But what if that doesn't happen? Are those decks cut off?"

"No, of course not." She flicks the dregs of her drink between the decking and unfolds her limbs. "There are service ladders. We can always get between decks in an emergency. I'm starting my shift now. Good luck with that baby."

She turns and walks away down the deck. She's not young, but there's something languid and panther-like in her movements. Her long hair shines against her back. Nerissa watches her stop to talk to Rachel, the girl from the laundry, and help her set up her bric-a-brac stall.

Nerissa scans the deck for ladders. There is nothing visible. She has seen nothing reaching beyond the normal stairway. She checks that no one is watching her and walks softly to the end of the deck, slipping down into the gap and behind, to where she first saw the graffiti.

STOWAWAY LIVES ON

It is still here. If anything, the coloured chalk looks brighter and more defined. Nerissa angles her pencil torch into the gap, knowing she can no longer be seen from the deck. She had not noticed it the first time, when she came in the night, but there is a curved, steel rung set into the wall. She shines the beam above it. Another rung. And another. Her eyes follow a whole set of them up as far as the torch beam will go. The space is narrow, but looks as though it would widen as she climbs. It will be like climbing inside a wall. Whoever put the graffiti here may not have come onto the deck at all, but climbed down and back up again, at little risk of ever being seen.

Nerissa is not good with heights, and she sees that one slip will send her down, sliding with her back against the wall. She can wait until the lifts are working again. But by that time, someone else may have found Molloy. She tightens the straps on her rucksack, pushes the torch into her pocket, and begins to climb. As she climbs, the shadows deepen. Away from the deck and not close enough to the next level, very little light is filtering in. The rungs are slippery against her plimsolls and her fingers. Her legs tremble. Soon the wall angles away, and she has only air and black space behind her, the rungs of the ladder reaching up above her as far as she can see. She may be able to make out a drop of light far in the distance. The space echoes with the hum of the descending ship. She rests on the ladder, afraid to go up farther. Even more afraid to go down. What was she thinking? She hooks her elbow around a rung and draws the torch from her pocket. All the time, there is a fluttering inside; the baby is agitated by her adrenaline.

There is a creaking, moaning sound that suddenly comes from all around her, and the *Baleen* lurches down. She's jolted, drops the torch, and grips where she can with both hands, flattening her body into the ladder. The torch clangs and flashes as it falls. She doesn't hear it land. The whole ship has shifted and tipped. She has never felt it do this, not since the first chaotic day when they boarded. The movements still and she decides to climb, her palms slick with fear. She does not look above or below, only to the next rung she must catch and draw herself up with. A metal lip appears above: a small opening through which she can see light. She hoists herself over it, shuffles through a tube-shaped space, and finds that she can stand. She presses her hands against something metallic, cool, and hard. She fumbles in the rucksack for the spare torch. There is a metal door in front of her. She tries the handle. Locked. Of course, the service ladders are only for stewards. It had been too easy to get onto the ladder at the bottom. The pipe is dark and hot. Shadows from the torch beam move towards her and recede again as she desperately tries the door. She imagines climbing down the ladder again. Will the *Baleen* jolt her off before she can make it? She lets go of the handle and stands looking at it. Then she sees it turn, from the other side.

Garden Deck

Antoinette is golden-haired, thick-waisted, and voluptuous. There are deep creases around her bright amber eyes. When she opened the steel door, she had been wearing a beekeeping veil, and only those eyes were showing. Her fingernails are crusted with soil. She smells of grass and honey. She is squeezing dry-looking oranges into a mug, twisting a knife around in them to encourage the juice. The Garden Deck is filled with strong, white artificial light, but Antoinette has taken Nerissa into the shade, to a wooden bench. She hears the sonorous hum of bees beside her, sees their white homes. Antoinette passes her the juice.

"I've topped it up with water. It's a bit sharp otherwise."

Nerissa sips, her heartbeat steadying.

"You're nuts," says Antoinette, wiping her brow. There's a dampness in the air that reminds Nerissa of the rainforest.

"I'm sorry. I'm just very impatient."

Antoinette pulls out some trays and starts planting seedlings. Nerissa imagines Antoinette is the kind of person who always needs to be doing something. She delicately pats the soil around the flimsy plants. She writes something down on a pad, moves the tray to one side, and starts another batch. Nerissa looks out over the deck. Ordinarily, Deck Three, the highest deck most are allowed to visit, is filled with natural light, being about three quarters above the waterline. There are a larger number of portholes here. Now it is immersed. The indigo shine of the ocean against the lamps suspended from the ceiling gives the impression of a lush, evergreen ballroom. There are squares of land for vegetables;

a knotty, bare grapevine; a patch of long grass that seems to be fallow, freshly raked ground ready for planting. A batch of manure from her animals stands steaming in the corner. Others tend the bees, bringing out combs from the hives. One woman brushes something yellow from the hairs on her bare arms.

"So, I saw him in the cabbages," says Antoinette. "You say it was a rat? Seemed massive to be a rat. And not so nimble."

"He's a Woolly Rat. They're more like—well, I don't know, really. Not like the kind of rats that spread disease."

"It looked like a dog."

"I suppose it might. Not a big dog. Sort of spaniel-sized. If you saw it quickly."

"Well, I guess I did." Antoinette looks sceptical and shifts another tray of seedlings. Out on the deck, there are rows of people in masks, spraying the ground.

"You already get bugs here?"

"That's fertilizer. We can't use strong pesticides; not enough ventilation. We use soap sometimes, that's all." She taps the edge of a pot and brushes her hands together. "I wasn't the only one to see your rat."

"No?"

"No. But I'm only telling you because you're asking. Because I can see you're concerned. And because it is your animals that keep us going with all the shit they give us." She laughs. "And because you are nuts and climbed up that ladder."

"So what is it you're telling me?"

"The Doubeks. They saw your rat too."

"Who are they?"

"Leopold and Rudolf. Father and son. The son works as a doctor, though he never quite finished his training. The father, Leopold, looks after the engine."

"So why the big secret?"

"There isn't one, as such." She arranges the trays of seedlings on the bench, moving them around until they are square with one another. "I let them take some supplies from us. Without tokens. And I don't tell anyone."

Nerissa frowns. "Food? Extra food? Why would they need that?" She thinks of Nick, and his words in the cupboard.

"No, not food. I give them sand."

"What for?"

"I don't know what it's for. I think it's something to do with the engine. Some experiment."

Nerissa rubs the edges of her mug and frowns. "Do the stewards know?"

"Of course not." Antoinette glances over to the masked figures spraying the soil.

"Why do this for them?"

"Listen, I probably shouldn't have told you. But that's why they were here, and they saw your rat." She sighs heavily. "It's for my daughter. For her pain. Rudolf gives me something for her pain. She means more than anything. And it's only sand. Nobody will miss it."

Nerissa has heard about addictions. When the floods were coming. People would take things to help them sleep, to take the edge off their fear. You didn't know if the water might come roaring through your windows in the night. And some, once they started, couldn't stop. There must be others here like that, making moonshine or eking out what they have left of their supply. Maybe what Antoinette's daughter needs is stronger, or she has an injury that pains her. Whatever it is, she knows not to ask.

"Look, I won't say anything."

They search the deck together, spreading the grass apart, peering behind buckets and pots. Antoinette shows Nerissa the trampled and bitten cabbages. They stand next to a pile of raked, golden sand. She shows her where Molloy went, where he gnawed through a wooden partition and disappeared through a small hole and into the ventilation shaft.

"He didn't look like he would fit in there, but he squeezed through."

Nerissa crouches down and peers inside the shaft. She makes out tiny, muddy paw prints along it. They seem to go in both directions, as though he had run up and down, looking for a way out. For the first time, she feels sad for him.

"I think I need to follow this pipe down."

"How do you know he didn't go up?"

"I don't, but there's not much farther up to go and not much food beyond here. I'd also like to talk to these Doubeks."

Antoinette draws back. "But they'll know I gave them away."

"I won't tell them. I'll just tell them I want a doctor."

Antoinette looks uneasily about her, and then rests her big palm on Nerissa's shoulder.

"You don't have to climb down."

"Are the lifts working again?"

"No, but there's another way. It will bypass Deck Five altogether, and take you to Deck Six. From there you can get the service lift to Deck Eight. Service lifts will still work, as they are more basic than the normal ones."

"How do I get there?"

Antoinette sighs, raking a hand through her corn-coloured fringe.

"You slide."

Nerissa sits on a ledge. A long, narrow tube, just big enough for her body, drops away beneath her like an industrial water slide.

"It takes drainage water away from the gardens. It's barely a trickle, because we control the climate and we need the moisture. It's steep for a while, and then levels out. I haven't done this. But I know where it goes."

As she speaks, she's wrapping Nerissa's torso in potato sacks and tying them loosely, to pad her out. She stands back, rubbing her hand over her lips.

"Look, though, I really don't like the idea of it. You could hurt yourself. Why don't you just stay here until the lifts are fixed? You can eat with us. Sleep here."

Nerissa looks down into the darkness of the tube. She has promised Herman. She feels as though the *Baleen* is shifting, pressured by the weight of something, straining underneath the storm, and that the lifts may be down for a while. She shuffles her legs out to the edge, feeling the moisture seep through the sacks. Before Antoinette can say another word, she pushes herself off.

Cities

The tube drops away from Nerissa, the trickle of water turning to a rush and propelling her forwards. There's a faint smell of mould, and the metal echoes and creaks as she descends. She grimaces at the feeling of her body being dragged away. She panics. How does Antoinette know this is safe enough? The smooth metal sides speed alongside her as she falls onwards. What if this tube pumps water back into the ocean somehow, and she ends up outside the *Baleen*, floating for a moment in the dark water, tapping like a ghost on a porthole and then letting her lungs fill so she and the baby sleep forever? What if the pipe ends fifty feet above the deck and she lands, smashed and broken on the hard ground? She presses her palms against the walls of the pipe to try to slow down. She cannot get a grip, and the high-pitched squeak of her flesh echoes away from her. She closes her eyes. Perhaps it is best to finish things here anyway. They might find her years later, when the *Baleen* is in a museum, or visited on the seabed by curious divers. She will be wedged into the pipe, jewelled with barnacles. She'll disintegrate at their touch.

Suddenly, she stops. The pipe has almost levelled out. It seems narrower, and she has to shove with her hands to move along it. Crawling would be easier, but there is not enough space to change position. She pulls out her torch and shines it forwards, struggling to sit upright enough to follow its beam. Farther down, the pipe widens. It is level most of the way, so she shuffles slowly, making progress only by inches. After what seems like an hour, her back cramped and fingertips hot, she shoves herself into the end and stands, unpeeling the potato sacks from her torso. She is on a ledge, greenish water trickling over. There is a great open space beneath her. Below, she can see the coppery bloom of various parts of the engine. There is a short ladder off to her right, the tiny, open service lift to the edge of it. Everywhere, the sound of dripping and running water and a creaking, groaning noise, softly churning beneath that. Above and below, she can see the edges of people's quarters where the rooms intrude into this strange, nowhere space. Nobody can see her.

The service lift opens with a clang, and she draws the mesh door shut. She presses nine, hoping to travel as low as possible into the engine room and find the Doubeks. The lift trundles down, revealing the backs, undersides, and edges of quarters as it goes. They all face outwards, the other way, for as much light and as many portholes as possible. She hears snippets of sound: raised voices, laughter, conversation, moans of sex and sadness. Smells of cooking and little wafts of steam rise to meet her. These are the sounds and scents of early evening on a street. Only there is no street, no softened tarmac, no one soaping their car or watering their flowers. No children tearing round on cycles or skates. As the lift moves into the belly of the ship, the slick walls scroll up, leaving the quarters behind.

Nerissa sees the writing dimly at first, and then passes her torch beam over it as the lift creaks down. The word STOWA-WAY is printed in marker all over the steel walls, and there are posters taped on with shaded drawings of a figure. The image is different in each. In one, he is a crude matchstick man, with lines emanating from his arms like beams of light. In another, he's artistically drawn with long, tousled hair, lots of colour, and lines of poetry written beside him. In some images, he has the face of a lion, or a bird. In others, the tail of a fish. The posters are filled with scrawled words. Nerissa only catches a few phrases as she descends in the dark, the thin beam of her torch flicking around the walls. *Stowaway is beautiful. Stowaway will lead us to the new land. Come and meet us, we'll protect u from harm*. He appears as a minor god, worshipped in strokes of ink. The posters are damp, their colours seeping into one another, the edges gradually peeling away.

The lift slips down again with a jolt, and she pulls the door open. She stands on a platform, which reaches around the edges of Deck Nine. There is a stairway leading down and various metal partitions, which she guesses must protect certain parts of the engine. They have small, padlocked handles on them. There is no sign of anyone, but she spots a mug, left to one side of the walkway, a thin wisp of steam rising from it. She heads towards the partition closest to the mug and sees that the padlock has not been snapped shut. She slips it from the handle, places it next to the mug, and pushes the partition slightly open.

Once inside, there is not the small, cramped space filled with pipes and gauges that she expects. Instead, she is slightly raised above a large, oval room. The walls of the room are curved and seem to be formed from parts of the engine, which, she realises, is immense, held here at the heart of the *Baleen*; it must account for about a third of the ship's total volume. At the centre of the room is something else; her eyes try to adjust to it. At first, she sees liquid: strange rivulets and bubbles. Then, as she watches for movement, she sees none. The collection of shapes at the centre of the room have edges, corners, shining domes, spikes, and they glisten, reflecting off and back to the copper of the room's walls. It gives them a pinkish hue. Ice?

But this room is hot, warmer than the platform she has come from and still wavers on. And yet these icy sculptures don't steam or drip in the burnished heat. She slides farther into the room to try to see more clearly, to interpret the glimmering forms below her. She feels a sense of déjà vu in this odd, industrial space with its frosty images.

"Can I help you?"

She gasps and steps back. A man of about her height, etched with lines, wearing a dark leather apron and hefty gloves, is standing right next to her. Has he been here all the time? She recognises him from Deck Five; his impassive face, his soft Central European accent. The Mender. He does not seem to recognise her.

"I'm really sorry. I was … looking for someone."

"How did you end up here?" he asks, pulling off one glove and then the other. He smells metallic.

"It's . . . a long story." Nerissa feels as though she has looked at something that should have remained secret and averts her eyes from the shining centre of the room.

"The lifts are out of order," he says simply.

"Not the service lifts."

His grey eyebrows meet. "No. But how would you reach those?" His voice is calm, like someone speaking through her sleep to wake her.

"I was looking for the Doubeks."

"Ah, well," he says, "you've come to the correct place." He makes his way down the steps towards the transparent, bright shapes. He disappears briefly beneath the platform as he goes. Nerissa hears the ting of his feet against the metal. She follows, unsure if she is invited. When she reaches the bottom, the last step is higher than the others; he turns and puts his hand out for her.

"I'm Leopold Doubek."

His hand is dry and warm. Nerissa takes the last step down.

"Nerissa Crane. We met once. You repaired my watch strap."

"Yes," he says, turning her hand over to look at Greg's watch. "I used to be a watchmaker. Not much call for it here." His green eyes look rheumy, rimmed with blue.

"So, you look after the engine?"

"Yes, with my son, Rudolf. He is also a doctor. He tells me all machines are essentially similar."

"And this is part of the engine?"

"No, of course not." He chuckles and turns to the centre. "This is just something we do, using our family skill: glassmaking."

Glass. Of course. The liquid, the ice, the shapes, suddenly come into focus. This is all made of smooth, reflective, lustrous glass. Most of it is transparent; some of it is etched with colour. Nerissa walks forwards, as if she has been given permission to look. Not only can she now see that all of this is made of glass, she also sees what the shapes represent: buildings. Towers and turrets; transparent domes; obelisks with tiny, pinprick windows. She sees squat, crisp little houses; smooth, long streets flanked with empty shops and connected with carefully crafted bridges. This is a collection of dazzling, miniature glass cities. She recognises the bulbous dome of St Paul's Cathedral, a few inches from the friable glazed strands composing the Houses of Parliament and the brown-tinged curving sheen of the Thames. In a tiny Venice, *San Marco's* domes are delicately traced with gold and white, its square smooth and empty of people. The Grand Canal is also empty, the slick glass tinted aquamarine. Leopold watches her taking it all in.

"This is Salt Lake City," he says, gesturing to a range of jagged, opaque-tipped mountains looming behind a row of shining office blocks. "And this"—he walks around to the other side of the glittering display—"is Prague. See, Charles Bridge." She sees. And the fairy-tale minarets of Prague castle.

"This is where we come from, actually," he says, crouching down as if he could walk its streets. The glass water under the bridge has been set in slight ridges, as if caught in a breeze. Nerissa looks at him, his eyes half-closed as he peers across the miniature cities, patches of silver and shards of rainbow lighting up his old skin. She does not ask him why they have done this, because she knows the answer. All of these cities have been underwater for some time.

She and Greg visited Venice once. It was only accessible by boat. The gondoliers still took tourists along the canals, each one standing proudly against a long, beechwood *remo*, pushing them above the silent city, the domes of *San Marco* just tipping the green surface of the water, the top of the towering

Campanile still above the water line. Darting fish reclaimed the narrow, cobbled streets, and algae furred the window shutters. What slid on beneath them was a ghost city, empty of its people, its rescued artworks hanging in museums around the world, anything left behind floating in flooded rooms or resting on the silty canal bed. In the *Scuola Grande di San Rocco,* most of Tintoretto's narrative paintings have been removed, leaving vast, empty patches of wall. Those too difficult to move still hang, with no one to view the fading expressions on the characters' faces as the colours gradually lift and bleed into the water. Leopold must be old enough to remember this city before it sank. He is creating all this to show people what used to be.

"I'm thinking about making Amsterdam," Leopold says, "but the bicycles are going to be tricky."

"How do you do all this?" she asks, her eyes everywhere, searching the cities for their details. Leopold walks into the shadows of the room, made darker by the luminescence at its centre, gesturing for her to follow. His movements are solid and strong, though he's a touch bow-legged. He has a big bunch of keys that rattle as he pulls them from his apron pocket. The edges of a small doorway appear in the shadow. He flicks open a padlock and pushes the door open, waving her ahead of him. He rubs his forehead.

"I must go back and lock the other door and get my tea. I am so forgetful at times." He smiles and is gone before she can say anything. Essentially, he is locking her in down here. But she has no fear of Leopold. The room is small and hot. A large pipe leads into what looks like an oven or a kiln. It has a glass window like a small version of a porthole. An orange flame, tipped here and there with green and blue, can be seen through it. There are various implements laid out on a long wooden bench, others placed on a shining white table: giant tongs; glinting off-cuts of glass, scorched black in places; jars of coloured powders. She pulls off her tank top and unfastens a button on her shirt. She glances back to the glass cities framed in the dark doorway.

Leopold is there, going around with a cloth, polishing minarets and domes. Has he forgotten her? She hovers between the rooms, over-heating, watching the flame flicker inside the kiln. She longs for water, just a drop. She fumbles in her rucksack for her bottle. She closes her eyes. When she opens them, she sees the dusty floor of the deck at an odd angle, tiny coils of glass like silver hairs shimmering against the wood. There is a pressure at her back, a dragging feeling. From very far away, someone says, "Oh, dear." Then all is darkness.

Molloy

is no longer in the ventilation system. He pads along the edges of Deck Five, cooler air on his fur, the softer touch of wood on his paws. He runs around the lips of the portholes, the camera taking in dashes of the dark sea. The deck is busy with feet: sandalled, laced, buckled, shuffling and striding around him. He presses close to edge, his thick fur rubbing against the wood and the glass of the portholes. He sees underneath the vendors' stalls, the bottoms of barrels, and discarded bits of cloth and paper curled on the wooden decking. He hears murmured voices, calls and shouts that he can make no sense of. He smells raw potato, cheese, oils, soap. The currents of these smells criss-cross ahead of him. He is unsure what to follow, where he will be taken. Nobody notices him. Nobody looks down and gasps at his fuzzy bulk scurrying along the porthole edges. His instincts are confounded. He stops, resting on a porthole ledge, tasting the air. The low vibrations of the ship carry into his paws. Outside, the blankness of the water is obscured by a shape; it drifts into view slowly, caught on Molloy's camera. He watches it come towards the glass. It picks up speed, and then bursts out like a huge flower, before shooting forwards in a long, slender white line. It billows out again, like a cloud growing. A deep grey flashes momentarily across it. It is reaching out towards the porthole. Molloy sees it as a giant hand, closing around him. He does not know the transparent glass protects him from being touched by anything in the sea. And yet, he doesn't move. He is mesmerised. The porthole is covered by something fleshy and pale. It attaches with a slight sucking sound: a weird caress. Molloy sniffs at the glass and twitches his nose at this quivering strangeness that has come from the darkness.

Port Mandelbrot

Nerissa remembers the letter asking her to join the *Baleen* as if she had only just read it. There was nothing left of the Institute, all their research was lost, and she couldn't bear to be in the city anymore, so she returned home. She had been given a tiny flat in a huge mid-twentieth-century tower block. It was three-quarters empty, and its open concrete walkways howled in the sea wind during the night. The bottom four storeys were underwater, and a rickety floating walkway had been constructed to take its residents to a curve of higher ground, where they could collect supplies and any post should it get through. Greg had been dead for weeks. She walked down the twenty flights of stairs, as she did each day (the lift long since broken), trudged across the sodden ground, gave her name, and was handed a four-litre bottle of water and a bag of bread and carrots, and, on this day, a brown envelope wrapped in plastic. She didn't recognise the writing.

Back in the flat, she read the letter. It was from a group who called themselves simply, 'the crew of the *Baleen*', and they wanted her to join them. They said they knew of her skills from the Mithras Institute. She was to look after a variety of domestic and zoo-bred animals, species chosen to be saved, many donated; an odd collection from surviving zoos and private donors. There were several vessels due to sail. Most would be privately chartered, their owners taking only the highest bidders. Only the super-rich would be saved. But one or two boats were selecting people on other criteria. She had been chosen for her expertise. All of this was confidential, and they would need a decision in two weeks. She should know: the next flood would not be like the others. There would be few survivors. If she wanted to come, she needed to be at Port Mandelbrot in three weeks. They would arrange her passage there.

She crumpled up the letter and threw it into the empty waste bin. She sat at the window until the light faded, turning from deep yellow to violet. If she looked from here she could pretend this was like any other gorgeous sunset in a coastal town; people walking their dogs on the beach, or getting ready to go to the pub. But she knew nobody was out there. There was just the glassy surface of the sea, its bloom of green algae mirroring the clouds, swallowing the daylight. Legs cramped from sitting, she stood to look at the Italy-themed calendar on the otherwise bare wall, flipping its pages back and forth, trying to work out how long Greg had been gone, how long she had lived in this empty room, how long she had to decide. She saw a letter 'P' circled in red biro. She flipped the calendar forwards. Two months and no more red letter Ps. She wandered automatically to the window and sat down again, stretching her legs along the sill. She ran her hand over the peeling paintwork, picking some of it off to reveal the damp wood underneath. She put her forehead into her hand, closed her eyes, and stayed that way for a while. Then she rose and took the crumpled letter from the bin and smoothed it out over the kitchen counter. It would have been okay to decide to stay, to stay right until the water reached the twenty-first-floor window, right until it rushed in and carried her away. But what if she was not just deciding for herself?

The sea was choppy the day she left. She saw it from her window, grey and frilled with white. She hoisted her backpack on, clipped it around her waist, and closed the door. The only thing she left was the calendar on the wall, turned to an image of a Venice canal. She kept her eyes on the concrete stairs as she walked the twenty flights, then she walked across the bridge and headed east to the pier. The first boat was tiny, and she was confused, but the skipper recognised the pass she held out and nodded. He whizzed them out to a small, stinking fishing boat, the waves slapping as they angled into them. The second boat had two crew, a father and son with hard, sun-scorched faces, and two passengers, an old couple, huddled next to a stack of turquoise crab baskets. They had an old-fashioned leather suitcase with a cracked handle. The woman hugged a glamorous handbag to her chest, but was wrapped in a bulky, padded anorak meant for a teenager.

They had to climb a ladder to board the big, rusting ferry. Nerissa was afraid she would fall, the weight of her backpack pulling her down. But hands came down, belonging to passengers or crew, she could not tell, many hands reaching down and holding her, virtually pulling her into the ferry. The old couple were so afraid to climb, they cowered in the corner of the fishing boat, the woman shaking her head and whimpering, her husband tugging her arm to persuade her, even though he didn't want to move, either. The waves got up, tipping them closer, but then precariously far away from the ladder. The suitcase was dropped and spilled its pale clothes over the filthy deck. The skipper and his son were shouting. Nerissa didn't understand what they were saying, perhaps because they spoke another language, perhaps because the wind distorted their fearful voices. She doesn't know if the old couple made it. She never saw them again.

She was absorbed into the crowd on the packed ferry. Every available space was taken up with luggage and people. Very few people spoke. A few babies cried. There was no room below in the relative warmth, so Nerissa stayed up top on the rough crossing, pressed into the bodies of strangers. There was a faint smell of vomit and sweat. Nobody would meet her eye, despite their closeness.

When she arrived at Port Mandelbrot, her clothes were soaked, and the sky was a livid, swirling purple, black at the edges, an odd, white light at its centre. The crush to alight from the old ferry was such that her feet kept lifting from the ground. She grabbed people's shoulders to avoid falling down and being trampled. People dispersed quickly on the dock, running to their designated boats, which were all completely different, some huge and white like cruise ships, others low and chrome-coloured, all designed for conditions that no one could fully predict. The old ferry pitched, yawed, and creaked in the growing swell. It would not withstand what was coming.

She found the *Baleen*, its blue name painted on the coppery hull. It was not as big as she had imagined, but some of it was below the water line. It was like a fat, short submarine, whale-shaped and studded with round windows. It looked almost organic; if she stared at it for long enough, she might see it breathing. It dunted and pushed against its makeshift jetty. She ran up to it, breathless, prickled by needles of rain. A woman with long, dark hair and broad shoulders greeted her at the entrance, taking her pass.

"You're just in time," she said. "We loaded the animals this morning and most people yesterday. We were worried you wouldn't come."

"But I took the ferry today. You said today."

"We did? Well, if you say so. The crossing is long, and it can be delayed. Perhaps you did not leave today. But you have arrived."

The woman looked up at the boiling sky, steadying herself with one hand against the rocking jetty, frowning as if this were just some inclement, inconvenient weather.

"Well, welcome. Are you ready?"

Nerissa looked behind her at the emptying port, the graffitied walls, the blackening horizon. She thought of Greg, gasping for air in the cistern, losing his life inside the underwater palace. She did not look back as she heard the clanging of the door being secured.

Daphne and Apollo

Nerissa wakes in a room with low, orange lighting, and pushes herself onto her elbows. She is lying on a narrow bed with a smooth white sheet loosely covering the bottom half of her body. She feels lightheaded. Her eyes adjust to the shadows. There is a man sitting in a chair to the left of the bed, bent over a simple white desk, writing something. Behind the desk is a heavy set of wooden drawers of various sizes, smaller ones at the top, with mismatched handles. On top of this are five cardboard boxes. There are various implements sticking out of the boxes, but she can't make out what any of them are for. She hears the light scratch of the man's pen. There is a chart on the wall. He looks up. His head is square and strong, his hair wiry with shots of grey close to his ears. He has a five o'clock shadow: the kind of thick stubble that will never shave smooth. There is a deep dimple in his chin. Eyes she has seen before.

"You're awake." His resting face is solemn, almost stern, but then his smile changes everything.

"Yes." She sits up farther, gently so her head doesn't sway.

"You gave my dad a bit of a scare. Dropped like a sack of potatoes, he said, and not near enough to him so that he could catch you. He's a bit of an old-fashioned gent."

He has his father's eyes, but very little else is similar. He pushes back his chair and walks over to her. He's stocky, thick-armed, but with elegant fingers. His chest hair fuzzes above his collar. He grins.

"I'm Rudolf." He offers a warm, dry palm.

"Nerissa."

"I know. I've heard all about you."

He walks behind the head of the bed, and she hears a tap running.

"Have some water. I think you probably keeled over because you're dehydrated. Or blood sugar's a bit low."

She gulps the water. Now he mentions it, she realises she's famished.

"You need to look after that baby. I won't even ask you how you got to the engine room with the lifts out."

"How do you know ... ?"

"You're just starting to show; I noticed when we put you where you are now. I should be able to spot these things, anyway, considering."

"You're the ship's doctor?"

He moves back over to the desk, like a polite bear embarrassed about its bulk. He brings his chair beside her.

"I didn't qualify, but I'll do. We should be giving you folic acid, classes, all sorts of stuff. But for now, I recommend a ton of spinach and avoiding risky manoeuvres and dodgy schemes. How does that sound? I'll even write a prescription."

She smiles. "Okay. But I am a bit confused. Where am I now?"

"I brought you to Deck Seven. This is an extra treatment room, for overspill. And sort of my office."

"And the glass cities, the engine?"

"The cities. You saw those. Beautiful, don't you think? They are nowhere near finished, though."

"You seem to do rather a lot."

He laughs from the belly, like someone very young.

"Glassmaking has been in the family for hundreds of years. So we do that. We keep an eye on some of the more mechanical bits of the engine, but ... they programme it." He lifts his eyes to the ceiling. "We just catch any snags. It doesn't occupy all our time. I don't have too many patients. Our ancestors made sea-creatures, plant-life, architecture—all glass—and sold them to schools, to universities. To teach people."

"But how do you do it?"

"All that heat from the engine. A little help from the Garden Deck for materials."

Nerissa doesn't ask about this. She gave Antoinette her word.

"Mind you," he says, stage whispering, "we're not supposed to. We haven't asked. When it's finished, of course, then … But I can trust you not to say anything … ?"

He puts his hands to the back of his head and looks at her.

"I'm starving," she says.

Leopold and Rudolf eat in a large, square room that resembles a kitchen from an ordinary house. There is even a cream wall clock, a slight crack in its edge, ticking away. The stove is the only incongruous element; it looks like part of the engine from an old train, with two square hot plates hovering at the top. Leopold dips a spoon into the stew he's making, tastes, and gives a satisfied hum. Nerissa sits at a round table. Rudolf tears her off a hunk of bread.

"It's a bit hard, but I heated it, so it's okay."

Leopold passes them plates of stew, topped with thick slices of carrot, and joins them at the table. Nerissa dips her bread in and eats. She can't remember the last time she was this hungry. Leopold looks up at her as he spoons stew into his mouth. Little flecks of it sit in his short beard.

"I'm sorry," he says, "for not catching you."

"It's not your fault."

"I didn't get to explain the glass. I was going to demonstrate glass-blowing. It's lovely to watch."

Nerissa thinks of a breath, caught in a bulb of hot liquid glass. A living breath. Rudolf tears a chunk of his bread and holds it up in one hand, plunging the other chunk into his stew.

"I wanted to ask you, Nerissa, now that you seem better, what you were doing in the engine room."

"I was looking for you two."

"Why not make an appointment?"

"I wasn't looking for you as a doctor. I suppose I was curious, about who cares for the part of the ship that keeps it going. That's not the only thing."

"What else?"

Nerissa sits back in her chair, chewing a piece of bread. She feels as though she has been away from the animals, from Herman, her own quarters, for a long time, though she knows it can't be that long. If only the sun or moon were visible. If she doesn't think beyond this room, she could be on dry land somewhere, the night sky crisp and fresh, just beyond the window. Her quest seems alien and mad.

"I'm looking for one of the animals. He's escaped. He's pretty important because he's the last of his kind. He also has … sentimental value. It seems you might have seen him on the Garden Deck."

Leopold casts his eyes around the room, trying to recall. Rudolf leans his elbow on the table.

"He's that important to you?"

Nerissa flushes, aware of how absurd she must seem. Rudolf looks impressed and baffled.

"I guess he is," she says.

"I know!" cries Leopold. "The creature that ran inside the hole. I just caught a glimpse of him as he disappeared. I tried to poke him with the spade.

"What kind of animal is he?"

"A rat. A woolly rat. From the rainforest, Bolivia."

"As I remember, he looked as big as a wolf."

"Not so big." Nerissa laughs. "But big enough. So you just saw him go? No idea which direction? Did you hear him in the pipe?"

Leopold and Rudolf look at one another. They are reluctant to disappoint, preferring always to offer something: food, solutions, and the ghosts of cities.

"No, no idea. He made a clatter when he went, but you couldn't tell."

Nerissa sighs, unsurprised but more disappointed than she imagined she would be. Tears gather hotly in her throat. She keeps them there.

"I would like to make you some coffee," says Leopold, rising and collecting the plates, "but there is a shortage. I have that rotten chicory stuff. I hate it. So bitter."

He makes a gurgling noise and clatters the plates into the sink. Rudolf rests his big head against his hand and smiles sideways at her, rolling his eyes at his father. She smiles back, the tears now swallowed away, leaving a dull ache behind her eyes.

"I have something," she says, remembering the orange jar, "in my backpack. It would make a good after-dinner drink."

The chocolate steams from their cups, filling the room with its scent. It feels as though they are celebrating something, long before or long after it is appropriate.

"Tell us something about yourself," says Leopold.

"Dad, don't interrogate her."

Leopold shrugs and sips. "No problem, I'm not. Just making conversation with this young woman."

Rudolf purses his lips and blows onto the surface of his drink. "You must excuse him."

"No, that's okay. There isn't so much to tell. I was born in England, in the south. I trained to be a vet. I got married. I ended up here."

"What interested you about that profession?"

Rudolf throws her a look again. She smiles and runs a hand through her newly cropped hair.

"I guess animals intrigue me. In some ways they are so different to us. But in other ways they're somehow the same. It's hard to explain. As a child, I was fascinated. I turned that into something to be interested in. I liked the diagrams, the insides of things, their intricacies."

She knows that none of this is quite what she means. She thinks about the different ways creatures move: the panther slipping into the pool at the zoo, the humpback whale rolling in the water. The opened-out rat. The eerily glowing rabbits. She thinks of the smells of musk and dung; of low, rumbling sounds and squawks and rustlings in the dark, of naked, blind things slithering onto straw.

"And your husband? Where is he?"

"He died."

Rudolf's face darkens and he looks into his mug. It is still strange to tell stories of the time before. There are taboo questions; things that nobody will ask.

"We came from Italy, before Port Mandelbrot," says Leopold, as if Nerissa had not mentioned any husband. "But we're originally from Prague. The family is. My wife has been ill for a long time. She was not living with us. She is being cared for. We've been married fifty-two years." He smiles. "I am impressed with that, and I hope you are. But she's not quite the same anymore. Doctors can't fix everything. But she's happy enough."

Nerissa notices his use of the present tense.

"Well, we don't know. We hope. There's no way of getting in touch," says Rudolf, shifting in his seat.

"She's fine," says Leopold sharply. He rubs his own shoulder, tilting his head to relieve the stiffness there. Rudolf is silent.

"I remember her as a different person," says Leopold, calm again now. "The one who remembers me. I think of myself as alone, apart from Rudolf here." He chuckles and slaps his son hard on the back, so that his mug of chocolate, halfway to his lips, slops forwards. Rudolf says nothing and glances away to the stove, as if to check it is turned off. He looks back to the small splash of chocolate on the table.

"I wondered," says Nerissa, feeling a need to pierce the thickening atmosphere, "if you knew anything about the stowaway rumours?"

Father and son glance at each other, both with their elbows resting on the table. For a moment, they look alike.

"I saw lots of graffiti," she says, "posters and things on my way here. And I've heard people talk about him."

Rudolf leans forwards and clasps his hands together. "People need these stories," he says, "an idea of someone like this. People have someone to talk about. To put up posters about. Then some hear the rumours or see the posters, and think it must be real. It's mostly kids, but also lonely people. Or people just trying not to go crazy, all cooped up in here. It's something to focus on, a fantasy that has become collective, that's all."

Leopold looks at his son, smiles. "There's one story, though," he says, "that I heard about the stowaway, one that I like and I would love to believe."

Nerissa expects Rudolf to say something, but he doesn't, just looks down into his mug.

"It began some years ago," continues his father, "in Italy. In Roma, to be exact. Some of the world's most beautiful things were crumbling: artworks, sculptures, ancient buildings. But it was still one of the most romantic places on Earth. The one we call the Stowaway was not Italian, though, she was Japanese. She was working there—"

"She?"

"Yes." Leopold sighs, impatient. "She. She was working there, translating Italian into Japanese for exhibitions and information. One of her assignments was to create audio recordings for the Borghese Gallery. This gallery had been preserved, and rich tourists were still going there. In one of the rooms, there was a stunning marble statue of Daphne and Apollo. You know the story from Ovid?"

Nerissa shakes her head, and Leopold tuts. "Really," he says, "it shocks me what young people do not know; what they fail to teach you." He sips from his mug, preparing his digression.

"Quite simply: Apollo is a god. He desires Daphne and pursues her. But she does not want him. Apollo is smitten, overcome with lust and will not take 'no' for an answer. You know, in those Greek myths, women were very much abused. Daphne tries to flee and Apollo pursues. How to outrun a god? It cannot be done, and she knows it. She pleads to the heavens to save her virtue. Her prayer is answered, and she transforms into a laurel tree, the leaves and bark closing around her before Apollo can take her."

The story feels familiar to Nerissa, like an old dream, but she cannot remember ever being told it, or reading it. Leopold leans back.

"So," he says, "there is a statue, a Bernini, made from marble. It depicts them both. Apollo reaches out to Daphne, and the sculptor has captured her mid-transformation. Her beautiful face. Her soft skin. The hundreds of tiny leaves closing around her and great chunks of bark. Leaves on her outstretched fingertips. Apollo's desperate face as she becomes beyond him. They both appear unfixed, as if the marble floats in mid-air. The sculpture looks impossible. The leaves are paper-thin. The flesh on their bodies looks warm and as if it would give to the touch."

"And the stowaway?"

"Yes, yes, I am getting to that. The stowaway sees this sculpture and it takes her breath away. Tears prickle in her eyes. And there is a young man there. He is tall and blond and holds a notepad. He turns to her and says, 'You know, when this statue was restored, we discovered if you struck the leaves with a tuning fork, they make a sound like crystal.' He turns out to be one of the expert restorers, and she falls in love with him, of course. He's Finnish, his eyes as pale as hers are dark. He's almost as young as she is.

"They spend a year, maybe more, together in Roma. While he restores great sculptures, she translates. All seems perfect. But, of course, it is not. Roma becomes wet. Sometimes it rains for weeks on end. The ancient ruins are suffering and cost more and more to protect. There are fewer and fewer tourists. Travel is so much harder than it was. The government is a disaster. Roma becomes poorer and poorer. It is so over-crowded with refugees because it will be one of the last places to flood. Nevertheless, locals leave, offended by the squalor, going elsewhere in Europe, to work. Protecting the art is no longer a priority. He says he must return home. She wants to come with him, but he is reluctant. And distant. Finally, he admits he has a wife and child in Finland.

"Devastated, she stays in Roma while it crumbles around her. She sleeps rough at times; with so many others doing the same she does not care. After some while, she is asked to join one of the boats. She has special language abilities that they need. She debates with herself: perhaps death would be a relief. But she decides, at least, to travel to Port Mandelbrot. When there, she looks at the passenger manifest for her boat, the *Beagle III*, checking for her name. Of course, she is listed. But she also sees the list for the *Baleen* and on that list is *his* name. She has not seen him for months, perhaps years (it is hard to recall as the days have seeped into one another). She has a permit, at least, and in the crowds and push, no one scrutinizes it as she imagines they will, and she boards the boat she should not be on. Then she hides away, vowing only to watch him. To feel better for being close to him, but not to reveal herself. She believes he has chosen the one he loves and it is not her. She lives a half-life, always in shadow."

Nerissa imagines her: a once-beautiful, dark-haired girl, slight and agile, crawling into the pipes, living in the gaps between decks, grabbing leftover food and glimpses of her beloved with his family. She is about to ask Leopold a question, when there is a sudden jolt, a pitching of the floor. They all clutch at the table. The mugs slide away from them and smash. The table moves across the floor and crashes into the stove. As they stand, Rudolf grabs Nerissa's arm and hangs on to a metal upright. Leopold holds the kitchen counter, his eyes darting around and his cheeks flushed. The *Baleen* travels steeply down.

The Baleen Descends

On Deck Five, the stalls slide along the wooden slats, their flimsy structures collapsing and clattering, pans and pots rolling away and resting against the portholes. Gus Duras staggers over the deck, only stopping when he comes to a porthole himself. He presses his back against the thick glass, watching the sticky spillage of pancake mixture oozing into the cracks in the boards. There is silence at first, everyone grabbing for a hand or foothold, then the sound of things shattering and thudding onto the decks, and a sound beneath that: low creaking, almost a moan, echoing through the belly of the *Baleen*. Then people begin to call to one another in thin voices, panicking as the lights flicker and dim. Gus, breathless, sees something white and fleshy clamped across the window and cannot fathom what it means. The *Baleen* is descending sharply, as if sinking. He wonders if there is a breach somewhere, if water is rushing in and dragging them down. It is far worse than the first day they sailed. He still remembers those relentless waves, the struggle to control the vessel, the command to lie helplessly in quarters and wait it out, retching with sickness and fear. He thinks of Marie. She has stayed in their cabin since the Laundry could not be accessed. When he can stand, he must get to her. His Marie. He must make sure she is safe.

He doesn't notice a grey shape, scuttling away from him, down to where the deck points itself, down towards the seabed.

In the Garden Deck the hanging lamps and leaves sway as if in a weird breeze. Antoinette watches the ground pitch and soil float up, scattering over them all like brown rain. Channels of water swirl and pool at the end of the deck. She gasps, clinging to the strut of a bean-frame; it breaks in her grip and she falls, flattening her body into the earth. The fresh scent of leaves presses into her face.

Herman clambers down to the animals. They bellow and squawk, squeak and growl. Rabbits thump a warning with their long back feet and fix their glossy eyes on the shadows. The larger animals rumble out their fear, some pushing their cages to escape. Herman tethers a nickering horse more tightly and then drags himself along the stalls, making low shushing sounds. His own eyes are wide, peering into dark corners as if to imprint each creature on his memory. *No more chances,* he thinks. *None of us were meant to be.*

Engine Room

The ship comes to rest, creaking and groaning into the seabed, nosing into the sand. It stays at an angle, the decks sloping away, but it is possible to walk gingerly, holding onto anything fixed. Amber lights flash their warning, but no alarm sounds. Nerissa holds onto Rudolf's arm. Listening. She is listening for the distant rumble of water, then its rush and roar as it comes to take them. But nothing comes. The ship continues to creak and moan, like someone with a sickness trying to sleep. Rudolf straightens up, letting go of the bulkhead. His father is breathing heavily.

"We have to check the engine," he says.

The ladder leans down towards them at the wrong angle. It is as though they are climbing the ceiling, but they manage to crawl into the engine room. The glass cities shine and glimmer in the amber light, but some parts of them are in disarray. Bridges are cracked; the edges of lakes scratched or shattered; the tops of buildings broken off. They are not destroyed, but they will never be the same. Nerissa sees Leopold's face as he takes it in. His eyes narrow and he swallows, but says nothing.

They go back into the room where she fainted. Rudolf has her hand in his grip, steadying her, though she does not need it. At one end of this room is a pulsing blue light she did not notice before. An old monitor is propped next to it with green text blinking on its screen. As they approach the light, she sees it is behind glass, as if in an oven. It looks like a globe or an egg, but it is too bright and too hard to focus on to know its shape for certain.

"Don't look at it for too long," says Rudolf. "It will hurt your eyes."

She obeys and turns away.

"Are there any hull breaches?"

Leopold frowns at the monitor, interpreting the script that rolls across it.

"Nothing at all. No leaks. No damage. But we've descended rapidly, and there's a lot of energy going to maintaining pressure. We're at eight hundred metres. She's holding up. It's as though we've been dragged down by something, caught in something." He passes a hand across his forehead and rubs at the bridge of his nose. Rudolf leans across him, studying the text, the back of his hand hairy against the plastic.

"I'd say the same. It doesn't make much sense, but …"

He turns to Nerissa. "Let's get you back up. It's too hot down here, and not safe."

Nerissa thinks it is as safe as anywhere. A low beeping sound comes from the monitor before she can answer. Leopold presses a button that looks like it is attached to an old spring.

"Yes?" The line crackles. Rudolf presses harder on the button and the line clears.

"Mr Doubek?" It is a woman's voice, one Nerissa half recognises. "Mr Doubek, this is the first officer. Do you know what has happened?"

"No, not yet. Do your instruments tell you anything?"

"Nothing that makes sense. No hull breach. We just began to descend. It's as if … I don't know." The line goes silent.

"As if something pulled us down here?"

"Yes. I suppose so." Nerissa hears the catch of fear in Darshana Hardy's voice; the fear of someone who has always understood everything and is now baffled. But then her voice stiffens again. "Find out what has happened. Report back to us as soon as you find a way to move the *Baleen*," she says.

"Where's the captain? Does he have any ideas?"

"He's already investigating this—he's gone down into the ship to see what's happening."

"Can't you control her from there, as you always do?"

"We can't. Nothing will respond. If we try while you try, hopefully we can come up with a solution." The line breaks off.

"I can't see what we can do," says Leopold. "We can't budge anything." His voice bleats out and reminds Nerissa of how old he is. How tired he seems. She is afraid now, not as she was when she came aboard, not as she was climbing up into the blackness or falling into the pipe, but afraid in a melancholy way, as if her heart has learnt to beat more slowly. But she pretends she is not afraid.

"I think we can start with something," she says. They both turn to her.

"We can take a look out of the window."

Ruins

Beryl sits at her porthole, leaning against its curved frame. She would normally be in Laundry, pressing huge piles of clothes or plunging them into the washers. Or she would be on her break out back with Shirley and Pam, playing poker for tokens, laughing. But with the lifts down and now her cabin listing at an angle and in disarray, she sits at her window alone. She is not afraid. She always feels as though she is on borrowed time. Since Edward died, she has simply done what others have suggested. She loves stories because she is not in them. She reads what she can get her hands on and listens to anecdotes and gossip. But today is different. She feels strange and wonders if perhaps it is starting to happen: Alzheimer's or something similar, those complex pathways in the brain beginning to dissolve and flake away. She has been staring through the porthole for some time.

Against the glass is the tip of a tentacle. There are two round suckers, part of a row, like the poppers on a duvet cover, but giant and ridged with tiny teeth. Every so often this tip furls and unfurls. Craning her neck, Beryl sees it belongs to a long, silvery, whole tentacle stretching back around the curved edge of the *Baleen*. She has looked along its length again and again, as if to convince herself of its reality.

The porthole frames a scene, the outside lights of the vessel casting blue shadows and forming silhouettes. She looks at this diorama and imagines it has been created just for her. Out in the distance is a dark mountain range, jagged and lumpy. Up close, a white crab with long, hairy arms and legs shuttles past like a wraith from a haunted tale. It disappears from view and then shuttles back, closer to the porthole, fingering the glass, tapping to be let in. It has never seen anything like Beryl before, with her big, startled eyes and her floral dress. Beyond the crab, in the middle distance, is the huge skeleton of a whale, its ancient architecture thriving with red, worm-like creatures, each crested with a white plume. Sea cucumbers plough through the sediment of the ocean floor, leaving trails behind them.

These are not the only things. She has been staring for a long time now, trying to interpret the forms out there. They are angular, rising from the bottom of the ocean, full of crumbling gaps. Whichever way she looks at them, she can only conclude that they are the ruins of houses.

Molloy

is crouched at the back of the food store. The tins and baskets, loaves and packets, have stopped falling down now. He tears at the wrapper of a chocolate bar and wolfs down a square. He finds a ripe cheese and chews it down to the rind, hiding in the shadows as Nick clambers in, cursing and clattering over the wreckage. Molloy's camera records his laced boots and the metallic sounds of the tins being restacked on the sloping shelves. Nick puffs out his breath, working quickly. Molloy watches his hands darting in and out of view.

Full of food, Molloy stretches out. Somewhere in his brain, the instinct which drove him to escape begins to flicker and fade. His DNA, bristling to be passed on, senses its limits and its ends. He is the last of his kind, wired to record only what a Bosavi Woolly Rat can see. His belly moves up and down against the raw wood of the deck. His eyes flicker shut.

Architeuthis Rex

"It's definitely a squid," says Nerissa. "A giant squid. *Architeuthis Rex*. But I didn't know they could be this big."

She has only seen a giant squid once before, and that one was pickled. She visited the Darwin Centre, claiming professional interest, but really on a whim. She followed a small group of tourists through the airlock and into the basement, barely listening to the curator. The room had no natural light, and she scanned the shelves for the spoils of Darwin's *Beagle* voyage lined up in jars, pickled like liquid photos, labelled in his own script. A hippo foetus curled up, like a fat, rubbery horse; the soft fur of a chimp in stasis, returning Nerissa's gaze; an iguana, iridescent and fixed. A library of creatures. A packed auditorium watching her breathing. But what she had not expected, and what impressed her, was the much later addition to the collection: the giant squid in its huge glass tank, around which everyone gathered.

Giant squid had barely been seen in the wild, only rising to the upper layers of the ocean when dying. There was a grainy film of one billowing away into darkness. This dead one was like a fallen god, a twizzled skein with a huge head, its two long tentacles reaching away and its eight arms gathered and arranged so all the tiny suckers could be seen. The curator spoke of its eyes, now collapsed, but which would have been enormous like hubcaps. She looked at its gelatinous, deflated form and tried to imagine it propelling itself through the darkness. It was a creature from another world entirely.

Now, a giant squid is holding the *Baleen* fast. They have been looking at it for hours, peering through portholes on all the decks they can access; scanning it with the rudimentary sensors on the outside of the vessel. It holds them in its fleshy embrace, pulsing slightly. They are in the empty school, in Deck Seven, looking through one of the larger portholes. This one frames the squid's huge eye. It looks at them. What it can see, with so much more capacity for sight than they have, Nerissa can only guess. Perhaps it can see inside her, or beyond her.

"It's so weird," says Leopold, thrilled, "If only we could go out there." The pressure outside is too great, but Nerissa also wishes this were a vessel of exploration rather than a glorified lifeboat. Out in the blackness, deeper than light, there are all kinds of life. The ship's outside lights are turned up, allowing them to see what is usually in complete darkness. A huge thermal vent releases a stream of glimmering smoke. Fish with hard fangs and lamps dangling from their heads move in shoals. A bloom of jellyfish glows with bioluminescence. Nerissa thinks of glitter-balls and discos. She peers out at the ruined architecture, the suggestion of walls now furred with weird red algae, the jets of steam rising through what could have been rooms. How long ago would this city have been drowned, and in what kind of disaster? Had the plates of the earth shifted so much that water had simply poured in and put it at the bottom of the sea? Or is this an illusion; do they long for streets and houses so much that they see them now in these squared-off rocks?

"Could they just be big corals that look like houses?" says Rudolf.

"I don't know," Leopold replies, lowering his glasses. "They look so uniform, it seems unlikely. I've seen similar ruins on land. It is possible with a catastrophic earthquake, a town might … I don't know. It would have to have been thousands of years ago."

The squid, gripping them, staring with its giant eye, does not frighten Nerissa. It comforts her, as though it has come from a dream or she's conjured it up. But the ruined walls of the empty town, furred with red algae and crusted with barnacles, fill her with dread. When she looks at them her insides feel hollow and the baby stills in her womb. She touches the porthole glass, tracing the filigree of bluish veins beneath the squid's white outer layer.

"It's huge," says Rudolf. "And it doesn't show any sign of letting go. We'll run out of reserves of oxygen eventually, so far down. We've got to repel it somehow."

"Why has it clamped on in the first place?"

"Beats me. Maybe it thinks the *Baleen* is a whale and wants to eat us."

Leopold is quiet. He sits down on a tiny school chair, a poster of the alphabet behind him.

"That's only legend," he says.

"What is?"

"That squid attack whales. That's just a tale. Why would they?"

He rubs his hands around his cheeks, glances at the squid, and then looks at the children's drawings pinned around the room.

"Something like this has never been recorded before," he says. "It must be because we descended too deeply, into waters we would not normally find ourselves."

"We had to: the storm." Rudolf paces the room, sweat beading on his forehead. "Anyway, we just have to get the thing off."

Nerissa rolls a blue crayon around in her fingers, feeling its waxy surface.

"We don't want to damage it. Who knows how many are left."

"There could be thousands," says Rudolf.

"Or barely any," Leopold says softly.

They talk for another hour. Nerissa learns that the *Baleen* does not have any weapons, but it has numerous anchors, deployable nets, and fishing hooks. The squid's vast mantle, tentacles, and arms are covering the openings for these. Darshana has suggested they deploy these to repel the squid, but if they are released, its flesh will be pierced. Nerissa is uneasy, and Leopold agrees. Rudolf tells them they are too sentimental.

"Isn't there something less violent we can do?"

It is Leopold who makes the proposal. Whilst the ship cannot propel itself out of the squid's grip with the squid attached, they can use the waste water vents to send jets of water into the squid's body with some force. If it lets go, they will put full power into the propulsion system and move the *Baleen* away.

"And the squid won't be harmed?"

"No, I don't think so. Just a little annoyed, I imagine."

"So, how long do we have, oxygen-wise, to get this thing to unclamp?"

Rudolf frowns. "With the number of people aboard, with the Garden Deck's reserves, I'd say a week, at best. If people are anxious, which they probably are, they'll use more."

Rudolf and Leopold return to the engine room, but won't allow Nerissa to go with them. She promises to stay safe where she is. She sits in the porthole by the squid's melancholy eye, ready to hang on if there is a sudden jolt. She rests her hand on her belly and feels its tight, unfamiliar curve. She can't remember exactly what the curator in the museum said about baby squid. When a squid has young, there are probably hundreds of eggs blinking their eyes as they develop, most destined to be eaten or tricked away by the currents. Perhaps one or two survive and grow to be as big as this.

The huge eye suddenly moves away from her, startled from its gazing. Now there is a gap between it and the porthole. A tentacle uncurls and flicks out. The squid is being pushed. Nerissa leans her head against the glass and looks along the curved edge of the *Baleen*. White arms are peeling away and bulging out where the jets of water pummel the squid. It releases parts of itself in rolling gestures, and then suckers them down again, trying to hold tighter. The ship gives an echoing moan, a hollow, metallic creak that Nerissa hears around the walls of the schoolroom, as it lifts and begins to rise. The squid blooms out, like a parachute catching on the wind, and seems to fall away from her, but it is Nerissa who is rising, the *Baleen* slowly heading for the surface. For a moment, everything beneath her is black except for the channels of blue light reaching from the ship down to the seabed. Then a thin, white line shoots up from the dark and opens like a hand, enveloping the porthole and the ship. The *Baleen* groans, halts mid-rise, falls slightly, and then stays suspended fifty metres from the bottom of the ocean. Then it sinks, slowly drawn back down to the seabed, wrapped more tightly than before in the arms of the squid.

Calamari

The children are back in the schoolroom. It's harder to stand up on the sloping deck, but mostly they sit. The teacher's challenge is to get them to concentrate. They are anticipating something, buzzing and chattering. Imogen is the only quiet one; she barely speaks, seeming distracted by her thoughts. One of the biggest portholes is here, and all they want to do is stare out of it at the squid, at the thermal vents spewing their sparkly smoke, at the structures that may once have been dwellings. So she has made this their lesson. The teacher is both repelled and attracted by the squid. If she allows herself to look at it, she stares for a long time, but it turns her stomach. When she looks away, it's as if she has been dreaming. She has asked the smaller children to draw and paint it. They argue over the paler colours, especially the tube of white, which they want to blob into the other colours. One of them spreads silver glitter over her drawing of the tentacles. The teenagers have been given the task of writing a headline newspaper article. She thinks this will focus them and take their mind off their fear. The teacher listens in, from a distance, to the class's conversations. They always seem to think she can't hear them.

Lost City Discovered is Imogen's headline idea. She's working with Tom, who has other ideas. **Giant Squid Eats Submarine: Only One Heroic Survivor**.

"I thought we could be a bit more subtle," says Imogen, sullen, pursing her lips.

Darcy laughs at her. "She thinks she's a journalist now."

"I want to be a journalist."

"Who's going to read your paper down here? What are you going to report on, that gross squid, some crumbly old city?"

"We won't be here forever."

"Wanna bet?"

"I don't see why we can't dive out," says Tom.

"Don't be silly, Tom; we're too far down. What about the pressure? We'd get all squished. Your guts would burst out your head!"

The teacher notes how quiet the smaller children have become, mesmerised by what they see through the porthole. One says, "Will we take the big octopus with us?"

"It's a squid, and we can't. It likes to live very deep down in the ocean. So we are just visiting it."

"When it looks at me, I feel a bit sad."

She crouches down to the child. "Why?"

Its great eye is visible beyond the glass, an eye too human for the teacher's comfort.

"Because it wants to talk to me, but it doesn't know how."

—•—

In Social, Nick and the others have cleared the kitchen and are cooking again. Some people are afraid to leave their quarters, or are still clearing up the broken crockery, the spilled food, and the collapsed furniture. But others are emerging, meeting up, finding their friends. The ladies from Laundry drink tea and play a subdued game of cards. Gus strolls up to the counter, Marie's arm tucked under his, her petite frame in contrast to his broad chest and comfortable paunch.

"Nick, can I borrow a spatula? Can't find mine since everything rolled off the stall. I know it's somewhere, but elle est perdu."

Nick rummages in the back, then hands a spatula to Gus.

"You okay?" Nick asks.

"Sure. Managed to salvage almost everything. Pancake mix is not easy to clean off." He laughs and pats Marie's hand.

"Gus," she says, "I'll go and see the ladies for a moment." She stands on tiptoe and kisses him lightly on the mouth. She looks back and smiles as she goes.

Nick does not smile. He is beating eggs into a dented metal bowl. He concentrates on them. "So much for our new world. You know what I'd like to do with that thing out there?" he says. "I'd like to chop it up and serve it battered. A nice calamari with a wedge of lemon."

Submerged

They remain for days on the ocean floor, oxygen levels falling, supplies from Garden Deck unable to keep up. Nerissa sleeps sometimes in her quarters, sometimes in the School Deck, where the portholes are large and she can see outside. The squid regards her with melancholy eyes, and she longs to run her fingers over its smooth, pale skin. The baby moves more and more; its touches are like bubbles popping. She looks at it from time to time on the sonogram. It is both deep sea diver and astronaut, approaching her as if from a great distance of water or space, coming slowly into focus. It is both a stranger and someone who lives inside her, and she cannot imagine a time when it was not there. She writes notes about the squid, draws diagrams, reads every book she can find, scouring the tilting decks for information. She and Rudolf talk until late, though the indigo light never changes, trying to find a way to make the squid let go. They have no other plan. Leopold joins them when he is not tending the engine, which ticks by on low power.

One night, after the last of the chocolate is drained from their mugs, Leopold says,

"If we had known what was down here, there might have been more hope, up there."

"What do you mean?"

"Most scientists thought the ocean was almost dead. So few mammals, a great coat of black algae blooming out to try and eat the pollution. And it is so deep down here; most creatures can only breathe nitrogen."

Nerissa watches the dark red worms shimmying in the plumes of glimmering smoke. A thickly armoured fish with a row of teeth like a cage and a lamp dangling from its head bumps against the porthole glass. She has seen a shoal of thin, string-like jellyfish collapsing their soft bodies into exclamation marks and shooting away. New inhabitants of the drowned city.

"When the lights go out, we all go out," Leopold mutters.

"What do you mean, Dad?" says Rudolf, frowning.

"Sorry?"

"About lights going out, what does that mean?"

"Ah, I don't know," he replies brightly. "Can't remember my train of thought." He stands up, resting his arm on a bulkhead to uncurl his aching leg. "I think I should get to my bed, really."

She meets Gus on Deck Five from time to time, still serving crêpes from his stall, which tilts precariously on the deck. The other vendors are there too, and they eye the squid suspiciously as they collect together what little they have unbroken or unspoilt and share it out. The children run around Social as if some new game has been invented, whilst their parents try to calm them to conserve the air.

"Ma chérie, you look so pale."

"You look a little peaky yourself, Gus. I think we all need to see the sun."

"Such as it is: that weak and dusty light somewhere behind the clouds."

"I'm sure it's still there."

"I can do a waffle, or a crêpe, but they are a bit dry, a bit bitter, unfortunately."

"The chickens are unsettled. They aren't really laying much."

"And Garden Deck are having trouble with the sugar. But I must admit, to look out there, I almost wish we could go diving, if the pressure would not crush us. There is life. It is teeming, as you might say."

And so it is: bursts of fish, a dance of strange worms and jellies, flashes in the darkness and scuttling feet rousing the dust on the seabed, all framed by the curling arm of the giant squid. It is as though the squid has thought: *You need to see this, let me take you to see this and you will think differently,* and has pulled them to it, as a child might tug its mother's arm to show her something important, something as yet undiscovered.

Molloy

has reached the very depths of the Baleen; he can feel the sense of a limit in the tips of his paws. The hole he's found goes down and down, and there is the sweet and bitter scent of human at the bottom; a mature male who hasn't washed recently. He likes the smell; he wants to see who makes it. Out into the air and a little orange light, deep shadows, sawdust and straw on the wooden ground, a good feeling on sore paws and unclipped claws. Molloy rattles in, thin and dusty, his skin loose and his fur grimed up. There is a warm blanket to catch onto and climb. There is softness and a naked foot, which he licks. It springs away from him and its owner makes a high, sobbing sound. Molloy crouches in the blanket and watches. The light on his camera flashes red, red, red. His rat eyes are deep and glossy; his nose twitches in the low light. He does not run. The man is looking at him. He unfolds his hands and reaches one of them out and touches Molloy's head. Molloy dips his head down, and gently back. The touch is good. The touch is someone in the loneliness. There is no spade, no shouting. There are no frightened smells or masks. Something comes towards him: a piece of apple, overripe, brown, its cells sugary. The apple comes in, goes down into the small belly. The hands wrap around and lift.

"Hello, little fella. I guess I'm not the only one hiding out, then."

Initiation

Nerissa has been sleeping in one of the smaller, infant schoolrooms. But tonight she wakes again as the baby shifts restlessly in its world of fluid. The *Baleen* hums, and the lights along its decks flicker on and off. She glimpses parts of the squid through different portholes as she pads quietly along the deck, trying to still the baby—the whorls of a tentacle, its big, intelligent eye, a glimpse of razor-beak. With their huge eyes, they can see in the darkness of deep water, where only blue light penetrates. They may live a long time; no one knows for sure. Food passes through their brains. In legends they battle whales and bring down ships, crushing masts and folding them into the sea. She knows they can move backwards and forwards, as if they have no behind or front. No past or future. But she does not know why this one clings to them, unblinking. It is peaceful here, in its many arms. If they are to die, down here, gradually becoming breathless, it does not seem so bad. But the loss of the baby would sadden her, now she feels its life is real and moving. Will she recognise Greg in its face? Or a trace of her mother or father?

She hears voices, close by, and frowns. It must be past midnight. She creeps slowly to the edge of the biggest school room, seeing a flicker of yellow light. The squid's giant eye watches her, turning in response to her movements. Does it know what she is? Does it care at all? The voices coalesce into a chant, and she presses her body into the shadows behind a bulkhead. She sees children, about ten of them, standing in a row, wearing masks. One mask is painted to look like a tiger; one is blue and white with a dolphin's nose. At first it seems like a party, a late-night game. The children look about thirteen, perhaps a little older. Some of the girls are a touch taller than the boys. Children about to turn into adults: boys with a trace of hair on their upper lips, girls with budding breasts. She smiles and is about to go back to the little room to sleep. Then she notices the basins of water, like the ones at the Letting Go ceremony.

She sees two stewards, also in animal masks, presiding. One has the carved face of a stylised lion, and her voice is sonorous and deep, as though it echoes through a cave.

"I am stronger than the bull," she sings.

"I am stronger than the bull," the teenagers return.

"I take on the spirit of the bull."

"I take on the spirit of the bull."

"I am all creatures."

"I am all creatures."

Nerissa draws back, pressing deeper into the shadows. The teenagers are breathless. Some have tears glistening on their ruddy cheeks. A steward in a beaked crow-mask, glossy with feathers, lifts a cloth from a box. The group audibly inhale. Inside the box are mice, soft, brown and white, their noses trembling at the feel of the air.

"Now, you must take one each, and you know what you will do," says Lion-Face. "This is your initiation. From this point, you are truly altered, truly one of the chosen."

The group line up, one after the other, to take their mice. The mice must come from Nerissa's deck. She was not told they were meant for this. The teenagers stand in front of their basins, their mice wriggling in their cupped hands, pink tails waving out through their fingers. One of the teens adjusts his mask. His hands tremble. Then each lifts a tiny blade and opens up their palm.

"Hold it by the neck," says Crow-Face, "as you have been taught. And just a quick slice."

Lion-Face smiles, her teeth bright under her mask. "Don't be afraid," she says softly.

And the first one does it, suddenly, with a whimper of disgust, the bright blood spurting over his hands and staining the white pelt of the mouse. He drops the body into the basin of water, and it blooms pink. Then the others do the same, quickly, not wanting to be last, not wanting to think about it. Some cry. Others smile after they have done it. The basins shine red. But one girl, in a grey cat-mask, stands frozen, staring at her mouse's beady eyes. Her legs shake. The lion-faced steward approaches, her lips gleaming.

"Imogen, this is when you become a woman, truly. All women experience blood, become accustomed to blood. One way or another. She won't feel a thing," she says, lightly touching the mouse's head. And she takes Imogen's sweaty hand, which holds the sharp little knife, and grips it firmly in her own, squeezing her fingers white. Nerissa sees Imogen look up into the lion face, her lips pale, her own hand held so tightly in another's, the quick flash of the blade, the squirt of blood. The body in the basin. Nerissa holds her breath.

"Now," says Lion-Face, stepping back to the front of the room, "everyone kneel."

Imogen crumples to the floor and stares into the water in her bowl.

"The final part of the ceremony begins. Repeat after us, and when the room is quiet, immerse your face in the water."

"I am part of the ocean, and with the ocean I am one."

"I am part of the ocean, and with the ocean I am one."

The teenagers obey easily this time, brave from their act of sacrifice, and plunge their heads into the stained water in their bowls.

Nerissa stumbles, nauseated and dizzy, from behind the bulkhead.

"What *is* this?" she says. As she does, someone behind her catches her arm.

"Nerissa."

It is Rudolf. He steadies her where she sways on her feet. The masked women turn, just as the teens lift their heads, dripping and bloody from their bowls. Crow-Face pulls up her mask to reveal Darshana Hardy underneath, her dark eyes unblinking. Lion-Face lifts hers away more slowly, pushing back the glossy red hair. It is Esther Mortimer.

"Nerissa, it's good to see you again."

Esther

Esther leads them up, via a series of tilting ladders, to a deck Nerissa has never seen. It seems to be just above or below Garden Deck, occupying a curved section of the hull. They enter through a circular, copper door. The chamber inside is also curved. It is white with pale wooden decking, and there is a copper and wooden structure in the centre of the room. This houses a number of small, flickering screens. There are two large ship's wheels. Nerissa cannot tell if they are decorative or functional; they look antique. At the centre of this navigation system is the stone carving that once hung in the reception of the Mithras Institute, its left-hand side, where the sun god Sol used to be, shattered away. There are two large portholes through which she can see the press of the shadowy water and the very tip of one of the squid's tentacles, illuminated by the *Baleen's* lights. There are two other doors in the chamber, tightly shut.

"Nerissa," says Esther, taking the mask from her head and putting it down, "it's been months since we last saw one another; we must talk. I know you have questions. But first, I want to show you something. Something I know you'll like."

Nerissa looks at Rudolf, who nods, surprised by none of this. He is gripping her hand, to steady her on the uneven deck, to give her an anchor. Esther is like a phantom come from nowhere, from a bad memory that Nerissa wants to release. But she is also Esther, perfect, brilliant, visionary Esther. Esther, whose musical voice once meant hope. She takes her outstretched hand and allows herself to be led to the copper door leading from the chamber. Esther unlocks it. Rudolf wavers behind them.

"I've charged you with caring for the *Baleen's* animals because I know your abilities; I know the precision of your care. And I had hoped we might rebuild some of what we lost, when the Institute fell."

They enter a pitch-dark room. It smells pungent; of grass and rivers, rich soil, a hint of piss. She hears breathing in the shadows.

"All of the animals are in your care, but I have kept something special here. My secret. Nobody knows about it." She switches on a dim light. As Nerissa's eyes adjust, she sees a cage, running the length of the room, and inside it, the shape of a creature, russet-furred, sitting with its head bowed and its long limbs folded around itself.

"Hello," Nerissa says softly, and it lifts its head. Its big grey jowls and its small, melancholy eyes turn up to face her. Man of the forest. He unravels an arm, uncurls his wrinkled palm and touches his grey finger to the bars of the cage, as if pointing at her, choosing her for something.

"Rufus is my special boy," says Esther, "but I wanted to share him with you. He has to be in here because, let's say, he can misbehave."

"Poor creature," says Nerissa, under her breath.

"There are things I must tell you," says Esther.

Back in the navigation chamber, Esther re-locks the copper door and gestures to a plush sofa, incongruous in its naval surroundings.

"Why didn't you tell me you were here?" asks Nerissa.

Esther closes her eyes and bows her head. She stays like this for long enough that Nerissa wonders if she'll look up again; it is as if she has been switched off. She glances at Rudolf, then back to Esther. Esther is now looking at her. She lets out a long breath.

"I was going to meet you soon. When the time was right. It was me who invited you aboard the *Baleen*. I wanted you to settle in first. And things, well, they have not gone to plan. This squid …" She gestures to the portholes. "She is magnificent. What I wouldn't give to study her … But, we are in her power for now."

Nerissa's head hurts, and a sob is rising in her throat. She thinks of Esther the last time she saw her stone-grey face in Istanbul, telling her everything was buried. She thinks of what she has just seen: white mice having their throats cut, a sad orangutan, lonelier even than she.

"I didn't sign up to be part of your sick cult," she says, "whatever on earth it is."

Esther smiles thinly and rakes a hand through her glossy hair. She looks at Rudolf, whose face is impassive. "I'm going to tell you what this is all about," she says. "It's not the way I wanted to, but that creature out there"—she waves to the porthole again, as a conjuror might—"has forced my hand."

Rudolf moves and sits beside Nerissa. He looks into her face, taking her hand lightly in his big, warm palm, as if she is about to undergo a painful procedure.

"The *Baleen* is a special ship," says Esther. "Everyone aboard is special. We may appear quite ordinary, but we are not. Everyone here, except for those over fifty years of age or so, is altered."

"Altered? What do you mean?"

"Your job at the Institute; you were caring for animals, yes, but also investigating transgenesis. Ways to make them stronger by introducing the genes of other creatures …"

Nerissa's breath quickens, and a low sound hums in her hears. She feels the light pressure of Rudolf's hand, grounding her, preventing her from floating away.

"As you well know, DNA is a language that all life speaks. Everyone here has enhancements to their DNA, taken from animals, from the gifts that they possess. The first generation are altered, like Rudolf here, artificially. Like those glow-in-the-dark rabbits. The children aboard are the second, the first to be born by two parents with altered genes: natural conceptions.

And those of us who are older, we're part of the original group of scientists. We're nothing special." She gives a short laugh. "We have passed our breeding age. But we know a few things."

Of course, it would be easy enough, Nerissa knows that. But it had always been forbidden.

"What kinds of alterations?" she says, her voice sounding far away, as if she is calling to herself from a great height.

"Useful ones. Strength. The ability to survive without food or water for extended periods. Resistance to bright sunlight, built into the skin. Ability to transfer pollen. To breathe under water. Resistance to extremes of temperature. Everything we need to continue after everyone ordinary perishes in the floods. A necessary stage in evolution. But we couldn't do it without the animals, without the things they have that we do not."

"So I was never helping animals … not, not really." The words bubble out. "I was only helping … you?"

"Of course not. If we don't survive, neither will they. You should not see humans and animals as separate. That is a view of the old world; and look what it led to."

Rudolf turns to Nerissa and rubs her cold fingertips. "When the Institute was lost, in that terrible accident, almost all of the research was lost. We had been building the *Baleen* in preparation for the floods, but we had hoped to continue to develop further, to perfect our science. The accident and the floods forced us to make do. We brought everyone we could, everyone altered."

Esther says, "We brought every animal we could and every scientist who worked with us. We can start again, continue to experiment. All is far from lost, since now a generation of Altereds will be able to breed, with no ordinary people to dilute the genetic changes introduced."

Nerissa leans back into the spongy texture of the sofa. The back of her neck is damp with sweat. She feels as though the upholstery is swallowing her. She looks at Rudolf, whose brown eyes seem suddenly alien. She slips her hand out of his.

"I don't see what I have to do with all this," she says.

Esther smiles again, and crouches beside her. Nerissa can smell the musk of her expensive perfume.

"You are my most talented. My most compassionate. You know better than anyone the value of all this." She takes Nerissa's hand. "And you are one of us. Why would I ever leave you behind?"

Nerissa snorts. "I'm not one of you. I'm just an Ordinary, as you call them. Smart, maybe, but human. I'm not part of your experiment."

Esther's teeth gleam. She stands up again, unbending elegantly from the waist.

"My sweet girl, of course you are. You were one of the first."

She walks to the centre of the room, running her hand along the surface of the navigation system, touching one of the wheels, now useless as the *Baleen* lists in the squid's embrace.

"I knew your mother, Leonora. We worked together in the early days. You were once our little embryo. I remember you in-vitro, when we made your alterations. You were a great success. Your little brother, he was not. Your mother became ambitious and tried something risky with that one. The pregnancy did not end well. She always pushed the boundaries, but I admired her for that."

Nerissa remembers her mother, her greying face and taut belly, her crying in the night as her father rushed her out to the car she'd rarely seen him drive, and never in the dark. It was the first time he'd left her alone in the house. The room shrinks and darkens around Nerissa. She seeks Rudolf's hand and clutches at it.

"Your father took you both away after Leonora died. He wanted nothing more to do with our project. Altered children normally know they are special. They learn of their gifts gradually; they are nurtured. But he made sure you both disappeared after your mother's death. Nerissa is not the name your mother gave you. Crane is not your surname. That's why it took me so long to track you down. Your father didn't recognise me at your graduation; he had met me only once, perhaps, more than a decade before."

Nerissa feels the blood tingling in her arms. "I have no abilities. You're mistaken. You said yourself Nerissa was not that child's name."

"No? Well, answer me this: have you ever been ill?"

"What? Yes, I'm sure …"

"Think now. A day off sick from school? With flu. A cough? A cold? Ever worn glasses? Got sunburn? And what about your climb to Garden Deck? Do you think an ordinary person is strong enough to climb that far? Agile enough? Or to ride through the water pipes?"

"That doesn't prove anything."

"All right."

Esther suddenly strides to the other copper door, her heels striking the deck. She opens it and slips into another room. Nerissa turns to Rudolf.

"It's all true," he says, not looking at her.

"Everyone knows. You kept it from me? All of you?"

He turns to face her, his blue-black stubble a shadow across his chin, his eyes brown and now thoroughly human, a trace of coffee-scent on his breath. "No one kept it from you. We don't talk about it often; it's just who we are. We all grew up knowing, had our whole lives to get used to it."

Nerissa thinks about everyone she has met on board, the panther-like movements of the stewards, Gus's strong, thick fingers, Marie with her quick, feline face, the woman on Garden Deck with pollen dusting her arms. She hears the sound of running water. Esther comes back with a bowl of water and two white towels.

"If you don't believe me," she says, placing the sloshing bowl into Nerissa's lap, "this will prove it. Put your face under the water and breathe."

Nerissa looks into the water at her reflection, drawn and dark under the eyes, her dusky skin without a trace of pink. She recognises her father there, in his last years, when he forgot to smile. Before she can speak, a hand clamps onto her neck and pushes her head into the water. She hears the muffled lag of liquid and lashes out with her hands, but the bowl comes up to meet her and her face is pushed lower, deeper. She gasps and the water fills her mouth. She will drown.

But she doesn't drown. Somehow, she breathes the water back out, and in again. It bulges into her lungs. It feels like air feels, only denser, and she would not be able to speak through it. Her lungs feel fat, distended, pressing against her ribcage. Her heart beats thickly; her blood seems sluggish in her veins. But she breathes. She does not drown.

As suddenly as her head was plunged into the bowl, it is dragged back out, water pouring down her face and neck. She retches, vomiting water and bile back up into the bowl. Its surface turns oily. Rudolf puts his arm around her, wraps the towel around her neck. Esther stands to her side, wiping her hands, her face grim, splotches of water on her blouse.

"Was that really necessary?" says Rudolf.

"Everything is necessary," says Esther. "Now you see, Nerissa, that you are one of us? You never discovered it because your father didn't want you to. But also because of your fear of water."

Nerissa thinks of her diving, of checking the yellow 'octopus', of the whales. Greg, diving that day without his tank on the whale run. Greg, drowning in the Basilica Cistern.

"Greg," she says, "was Greg altered? Could he breathe under water, like me?"

Esther's face softens. "No," she says, "Greg was ordinary. Greg was not altered. He was fearless, but not because of anything special. When I realised how much you loved him, I knew there was a problem."

A sob escapes Nerissa's throat, and big tears well up into her vision. Now the tears have begun, she feels they may not stop. Despite her abilities, she will drown in them.

"I tried," says Esther, "to get you together with someone altered, as we do with all young Altereds. To bring you into the fold. To ensure you passed on the genes. Chairil was my idea, in Borneo. He was quite lovely. But events beyond my control put paid to that. And Greg just always seemed to be there, popping up, distracting you. You would only come to the Institute if he came too, so I allowed it. I knew we would have to tackle it, though."

"Why couldn't I be with someone normal?" Nerissa says, her sobs choking her.

"You could. But if you had children, they would only have a fifty percent chance of carrying the altered genes. If we let everyone do that, our new race would be slowly watered down. But the *Baleen* is the solution to that problem. There are no ordinary people who can breed now. You were always the exception, Nerissa. In everything. Clever Nerissa: the lovely snag in the plan."

The deck is quiet for a moment, the only sound the muffled gasps of Nerissa as she cries.

"I don't want to be here," she whispers. "This isn't where I belong."

"Greg wanted you to be here, Nerissa."

"What do you mean?"

"After the accident at the Institute, I told him of our plans. Of the *Baleen*."

"But he was—"

"Not dead. Lucky as ever."

Nerissa says nothing, only stares at Esther, the feeling draining from her body, her sobs caught in her throat.

Esther continues, "He had to go to hospital, with others who were injured. He was in poor shape. I told him the truth then. I was afraid for your future. I said there could be no place for him on the *Baleen*, because he was not altered."

"He would not have believed all this. He would have spoken to me."

"And seen you both die in the floods? His love for you was real, more than his love for his own life."

"He didn't think the floods …"

"After the accident, after almost drowning in the Cistern, he knew what was coming."

"He would never agree to lie to me," cries Nerissa, remembering the sirens, the photos blooming dark red in their trays of liquid. The baby shifts inside her.

"The ironic thing is, he survived a lot of things. He had no alterations, but he lived as if he had. Great shame, really."

"You're lying to me."

"What difference would it make, anyway?"

Nerissa sinks into the sofa, which holds her in its dumb, fat arms. Something is coming over her. It muffles her senses. The hum around her grows loud and fuzzy, and the room blurs as if smudged by a thumb. She hears voices from far off trying to reach her through the thickness of water.

Rudolf

Nerissa is lying in her cabin. She is loosely covered with a blanket. The strip of material that hangs over her porthole is still there, but she can see behind it to the water outside and the strange ruined city that haunts the seabed. Rudolf sits beside her. Her lips are dry and stuck together, and the angle of the ship has brought on her nausea.

"Nerissa," Rudolf says, as he lifts a cup of water to her lips, "I'm sorry about all this."

She doesn't speak. She looks at his face, his broad shoulders and the backs of his hairy arms. His animal features are not visible, but deep within his DNA. He is no more werewolf than she.

"How could I not know?" she whispers to him.

"How would you?" he says. "Perhaps if you had been less afraid of water, but … We grew up knowing. My father was one of the first scientists, the pioneers. He didn't even know what I'd experience. When puberty hit, well, it wasn't the same for me as ordinary boys, and it was bad enough for them. I had the same things, but other things too. Hot flushes, chills, skin flaking off in sheets, insects all over me in summer, especially bees, horrific dreams. That's why they have Initiation now. It seems nasty, but the ritual helps."

Nerissa turns her face away from him, pressing it against the porthole. She thinks of them all down here in their compartments: boxes in a round metal tube with its thick metal walls. Its unfinished wooden decks. Their silly market and their social games. Her insistence on trimming her hair. On eating.

On getting out of bed. Animals stinking below decks. Keeping them alive or watching them die. Going mad in the half-light. Dreaming of air and of soil underfoot. Of wind. Most of all, of wind pushing in from the hills and trying to lift her from her feet. Slapping her face. Bending the trees. To stand once more in the wind just for five minutes. Would she die for that? She could have, if she'd wanted. She had her chance.

"We can't swim out of this, if that's what you're thinking. The pressure. We're still mammals—they can't survive at these depths. They have to breathe air from time to time."

"Mind reading is not one of your abilities, then. I wasn't thinking that. I was thinking, what if this baby is not one of you? Of us. What then?"

Rudolf says nothing for a moment. Then, in a low voice, he answers, "She told me if it's not, then it can't stay. The whole point is to create a new, strong race, designed to survive whatever—"

"And what will she do? If it's not?"

He swallows and looks at her.

Her face is turned to the sea. The sea that knows nothing. The careless sea. Her voice comes out quiet and dull. "So, it's fifty-fifty. Tails I win, heads I lose," she says. She feels Rudolf's palm, cool against her cheek. He turns her face gently towards him.

"I won't do it, Nerissa. I did not sign up for this." His voice comes out in a growl. "I'd rather take my chances, and leave this ship."

"And how," she says, sitting up, grabbing his arm, "are we supposed to do that? There is this slight problem of a giant squid. Of being trapped down here."

He takes both her hands, curling her fingers into his.

"I'm afraid I have more revelations," he says.

Stowaway

Nerissa is in her workroom with the three men: Rudolf, leaning on the counter; Herman, standing straight, not able to meet her gaze; Leopold, crumpled in her reading chair. She feels lightheaded, empty of tears.

"Dad," Rudolf squeezes his shoulder, "are you all right?"

"Just tired." He looks up with watery eyes. "I've been trying to fix everything. Most of Vienna is broken. I may have to make it again."

"At least nobody was seriously hurt," says Nerissa. She smooths her hand over her belly. Rudolf cracks his knuckles in the silence, exhales hard, and looks straight at Herman.

"Listen," he says, "I got us all here because there is something you need to know."

Herman raises his hand, reaching towards Rudolf as if to stop him, but does nothing, only keeps the hand there, as if he might catch Rudolf's words mid-air. Rudolf narrows his eyes.

"Look, Herman, I think at this point we might as well come clean."

Leopold frowns. "What do you mean, Rudolf?" he says, looking from him to Herman. Herman looks down at his feet.

"I think it's best that you see for yourselves." He heads for the ladder that leads down to the animals.

Leopold is shaky on the ladder; Rudolf stands below him, one arm poised to catch him. Herman steps ahead with his torch, the shadows of the animals rising up around them like paintings in an ancient cave. The dull light has quietened all but the nocturnal creatures, who blink and scrabble in the darkness.

Herman waits for them at the end of the deck, and then disappears around a corner that Nerissa did not know existed. They all follow, turning left after him. He clears some straw from the ground and lifts a metal handle. A hatch opens below him. He shines the torch-beam down a set of stairs.

"This is Deck Thirteen," he says.

"There is no Deck Thirteen."

"Yes, there is," says Rudolf, and begins to climb down the ladder.

Nerissa's eyes adjust. There is a different kind of light down here, yellow, like the glow from a bedside lamp. This is a long room with a ceiling so low they have to dip their heads. Pipework etches the walls and ceiling. There is a damp, metallic smell. The floor is bare and clean as if swept. She sees a makeshift bed along the end wall, a shelf with a few books and tins of food. A man is sitting on the bed, fully dressed, on top of the cover, reading. He rises as he sees them over the top of his book, and stands slowly. His eyes are wide with alarm.

"Herman?"

"It's okay, James, these are friends. It's, it's just with things the way they are, Rudolf thought it time to ask for your help."

The man, James, is wearing a uniform: a blue jacket with a symbol on the lapel, and dark trousers. Instead of a collared shirt underneath, he wears a grubby white T-shirt. The clothes hang off him. His feet are bare. He has a short, scrubby beard, and his hair is long, curling at the neck. His eyes are a striking blue, a slight droop to one eyelid. Nerissa moves towards him. She knows this face; she has seen it somewhere before. The voice is different, less clipped, less refined, but—

"Captain Holmes," she breathes, seeing an image of the clean-shaven face and perfectly combed hair from the ship's monitors.

"Enchanted," he says, offering a tired, charming smile and reaching out a hand. She clasps his cool fingers.

"I don't understand this, Rudolf." Leopold holds his son's arm, steadying himself. Captain Holmes sits down on the edge of the bed and looks up at Rudolf.

"Herman?" says Nerissa. He will not look at her.

"James," Rudolf says with a sigh, "I've told them because we can't really go on like this, stuck down here. We have tried everything. You might be able to help."

"What's going on?" says Nerissa.

"This," says Rudolf, "is your stowaway."

"It's a long story," says Holmes, "so I'll try to tell you only what matters."

Nerissa sits on a barrel, Leopold on a bag of animal feed, Rudolf and Herman on the bottom two steps of the ladder. Holmes looks at each of them and sighs, physically tired by his narrative before it has begun.

He tells them he was one of those kids: always perfect. Top dog. He did well in school. He might have been the only Altered there. Instead of feeling like an outsider, he loved it, excelling in everything: maths, science, sport. Confidence made him popular, especially with girls. His altered state made him feel invincible, like the worst kind of cocky teenager. He grew up on the coast, loved sailing, and adored the sea. He loved the way it changed, its moods, the way it ate the light from the sky and glowed with all its colours. The way it wanted to fight you one minute and buoy you up and soothe your soul the next. So he became a captain. Cruise liners. The older women would pay him to be with them whilst their even older husbands played mini-golf on the top deck. They were floating cities, triple the size of the *Baleen,* so easy to captain they sailed themselves. He barely felt the ship beneath his feet, though he determined its course. And that may have been part of the problem.

"One night, cruising in the Mediterranean, something went wrong."

He pauses, his eyes blank as he looks into the past, back at scenes they can only just imagine.

It was already too late when he awoke. He had felt no juddering through the ship, no impact. No one on shift seemed to have any warning. Had they hit something? It wasn't certain, but the ship was listing, sinking, filling up fast, and nothing anyone tried could help. He was groggy, hung over. He panicked, running up the listing decks. Some people were screaming, others dead silent, mouths set, trying to get out.

"I was too afraid to stay with my ship."

He stops and presses the heels of his hands into his eyes. When he begins again, his voice is quieter.

He tells them how he made it to the hull. He slipped into a line of passengers gingerly walking to one of the few lifeboats they could access. It was pitch-dark, only tiny pinpricks of light stretching away on the huge, tilted hull. He held the arm of the person in front of him. Someone clung to his hand. He did not help. He hid among those he was supposed to rescue, or die with.

"I wanted one thing: to save myself. When I could, without being seen, I simply jumped in. I knew I wouldn't drown. I came to my senses a few weeks later. Fear had overtaken me that night. It was unforgivable. I was arrested. I was glad about this. *Lock me up,* I thought. *I deserve nothing.* But the investigation proved there was something wrong with the ship. The company was sued. I was only guilty of cowardice, no crime in my country, but a terrible dishonour if you are a sea captain."

He sighs and rests his head back on the wall to tell them about the aftermath, as if he can't bear to remember but must. After the accident, he lived alone. Days seemed to stretch out ahead in a long, grey strip. He heard the sea and wind and screaming every time he tried to sleep. He saw figures walking through tipped decks, climbing stairs gushing with water. When he looked into their faces, they had hollow, black eyes. He wanted to crawl out of his own skin. Then the letter came.

The four, listening intently, look at one another. They had all received such a letter. They all remember where they were when they read it. Nerissa narrows her eyes, watching his face. What is he doing here, aboard the *Baleen*? He seems a terrible choice for a captain. She does not like the way he rakes his hand through his dull hair, the way he smiles wryly before he speaks.

"They wanted me to captain the *Baleen*. They wanted someone who could sail, but would also understand her hybrid qualities—her submarine half. I had engineering talents, they said. I had experience. This was a special ship, a little different from the others. Did I know what was coming? Did I understand only a chosen few would survive? They knew all about me; they seemed to know everything. They wanted to offer me redemption. I was to help them build the *Baleen*. I was to be a saviour of lives."

He looks up at each of their faces, watching for a reaction.

"I had nothing to lose at all. And maybe I had something to gain. I would be among Altereds like me. Part of a new race. That's what they want."

"So what are you doing down here, hiding in the dark? What went wrong?" asks Nerissa.

Holmes sighs, shuffles back on the bed and leans against the wall.

"I did not realise, not fully, what their intentions were. They had given me a second chance; I owed them my life, really. You remember the day we boarded, the day we set sail? The ship was barely finished. The sea was in a rage—I had never seen it that way. I thought, *They're right, it will destroy everything. Only those on the boats will survive*. And for weeks after, the sea was grey and blank, as if sulking after a tantrum. And we were thriving, working as a community, growing crops, making friends. I thought, *Only a vessel this small, with so few people, can make a group work in harmony. A village under the sea*. And when we found land, we would be bringing our strong genes back into the world. Everyone would be better off if we made it.

"After a few weeks, maybe months, I saw something on the horizon. The top of a mountain or hill, just the very tip. I was alarmed, of course, but we navigated around it. It had to belong to a landmass—our instruments are not perfect, but they told me that much. Even just a tiny island."

Nerissa holds her breath.

"I was elated, of course. This was a sign that land had survived. There could be more. We could be close to landing somewhere. Seeing what remained. Putting something back together. I reported it, but the reaction was not what I expected. 'It is meaningless,' they told me. 'It's just the tip of a very high mountain. Nothing could live there.' They would not be convinced. They dismissed me.

"Some weeks later, I picked up something on the instruments, and then I went up to see. A much bigger landmass, the edge of a coast. And that's when they told me what you know." He sighs again, and closes his eyes.

"Told you what?" asks Nerissa, who does not know.

Holmes's face darkens. He looks at Rudolf, who nods. Leopold reaches out and grabs Nerissa's hand.

"That Esther, and those she keeps close, the stewards, do not want us to find land. That I must steer away from all signs of it. That no one aboard must see it, ever. At first, I didn't understand, but it came into clearer and clearer focus. They were gentle as they told me. They want us to stay here, to create the perfect community, unsullied by the outside world. A generation of people will be born at sea to be moulded as they wish. Altereds must breed only with Altereds. To fast-forward evolution. And only then would they consider landing, when any survivors of the floods, any Ordinaries with their inferior DNA, have perished, fighting each other for resources. The flood, for them, is a chance to wipe the slate clean. And they have chosen us to join them.

"I did what they asked at first. But then, I thought, *I am being a coward again. This is no redemption*. I couldn't convince myself this was the right thing. I would not captain a ship of lies."

"That's a bit melodramatic, James, don't you think?" says Herman.

Holmes gives him a wry smile. Nerissa looks at Holmes with his swept hair greasy and unkempt, his pouchy, darkened eyes. He's arrogant, but defeated. Somehow, she wonders if he has learned anything about himself at all. She feels lightheaded and sways slightly where she sits. Things are a little worse than even she imagined. She hears him continue to speak, as if from a distance.

"I refuse to steer her away from land. Esther can steer the ship herself, see how far she gets. She would have no problem killing me, her and her cronies. They'll do anything for her. So, I thought of the stowaway stories. In a sense, they gave me the idea. I could inhabit those stories, live that way. No one would imagine a captain to stow away on his own ship. I hid for weeks in the pipe-work, the edges of decks, tiny passageways. I lived like a stowaway, stealing food. I couldn't escape, I couldn't do much, but I could refuse to be at the helm while the ship was steered away from land. I wasn't very good—I was seen sometimes, but people only caught glimpses of me. They had no idea who they had seen. They could imagine whatever they wanted. It was Herman who caught me. I had injured myself, scraped the skin of my leg climbing down a chute. It was turning nasty. I had found the deck with the animals, thinking that was the safest place; none of them could reveal me. I stole their feed and kept warm in their straw."

Herman smiles, looks at Nerissa for the first time, and says, "I was suspicious of how much the rabbits were eating. When I found him, he was delirious with infection and fever, so I went for the doctor. I didn't realise who he was."

"Why didn't you tell me?" says Nerissa. "I could have helped him as well. I have access to drugs."

Herman looks at her with a gentle smile on his lips. "I thought you would go straight to them and they would hurt you, and I could not let that happen."

Nerissa is about to speak, when she feels something furry bump against her leg. There, on the deck, snuffling, thin and dishevelled, is Molloy.

"Ah, yes," says Holmes, "I was going to ask you about him."

Superhighways

Captain Holmes is wolfing down a plate of fried eggs and bread, slouched by the sink in Nerissa's workroom.

"Well, at least that bald hen is good for something," says Herman. He is stroking the top of Molloy's grey head, running his hand tenderly along the dusty fur. The camera, still attached, focuses in and out on Herman's gnarly knuckles. Nerissa listens to Molloy's heartbeat, picks his legs up one by one, bending them this way and that.

"That's a pretty big rat," says Holmes, mopping up yolk from his plate.

"It's not really a rat, not as we know them. More of a small mammal."

"Why is he so tame? Is he domestic?"

"No," says Nerissa. "It's just that their species didn't have contact with humans. They don't think we pose any threat. They are quite social animals; they quite like humans."

"Like dodos."

"Like what?"

"The dodo. Pretty friendly, and rather tasty, apparently." He takes another bite. "So if it's friendly, why did he run away?"

"I can only think he was looking for a mate. I guess we weren't able to bring one with us. His time of the month, you know."

Holmes frowns, rinsing his plate under the tap. The water sputters on and off.

"What's that thing on his head?" he asks.

"A camera. We can't figure out a way of removing it without hurting him."

Holmes peers into the camera, tickling Molloy behind the ears to keep his attention. The camera takes in the captain's nostrils, his large blue eye, the lines on his forehead.

"Someday," says Holmes softly, "we'll get a look at the wonders you've seen. Someone will."

"How is he?" asks Herman.

"A bit thin, a bit dehydrated, but he'll live," says Nerissa. "Why don't you settle him back down, feed him?"

Herman gives a little salute and gathers Molloy in his arms.

Nerissa and Holmes pull stools up to either side of the metal table, she balancing on the edge of her stool rather than sitting. He rolls out a piece of grubby, frayed heavy paper with a schematic of the *Baleen* on it.

"I carry this everywhere," he says.

She feels as though she has climbed and shimmied through its arteries, explored its bones, its belly, and the engine at its heart. But she has never seen the ship whole and flattened out in a schematic like this.

"It has a special kind of reactor at its core. It is small, though, not like the kind on a military sub. It's not intended to be used for any great length of time. It works differently. This is a ship first and foremost, for sailing. None of us even know exactly how the reactor works. Well, maybe Leopold does, but if he explained, we probably wouldn't understand. But that doesn't matter. We don't need to."

Nerissa wrinkles her nose, unconvinced. She looks at the bulbous front of the *Baleen*, its long, narrow stern tapering to a point.

"Most of the stern is functional. Whilst the workings of the ship are in its centre—we live around the engine—the stern propels us forwards. The bow is sort of the brain, telling it how to happen and when. And the squid, it's wrapped around us at the widest point."

He takes a stubby pencil and draws a crude image of the squid and its tentacles embracing the hull.

"Rudolf and Leopold say it won't let go when we try to push it off, and here"—he prods the paper—"is the release for the anchor. She's completely covering that up. He or she. When they try to use it to repel her, they get a malfunction warning, and it jams. So we can't force her off."

"So?"

"So, we have to think differently. Can we lure it away?"

"With what? We can't go outside; the pressure will kill us and crush most objects. Isn't the key to this trying to figure out why she's clamped on in the first place?"

Holmes rests his chin in both hands and puffs out a breath.

"Seems like an attack. We are in its territory and it's defending itself."

"Then why grab us again when we move away from it?"

They go back to the encyclopaedia, looking for clues in smaller squid species and their behaviour, ploughing through myths and legends as if their faulty logic might hold insight.

"I'm even looking at vintage sci-fi now," says Nerissa, reading out a quote from an Arthur C. Clarke story: " 'The tentacles seemed strings of luminous beads ... or the lamps along a superhighway ... ' "

"What's a superhighway?"

"I suppose those great long roads, before we stopped using cars."

Nerissa thinks of her father, repairing cars for those rich enough to take them out from time to time. He took her out once, to test a revamped engine, just before dawn, the lights streaming past the window as they flew over the bridge. Her eyes could not keep up. She hadn't been able to tell if the clouds were moving out over the river or puffed up and motionless as they sped by. Her father had not looked at her but ahead at the empty road, a slight smile turning up his lips. The lights were blue and green and golden, studding the empty highway, curving away over the hills and reflecting on the water in smudged lines. To imagine the squid's tentacles in this way suggests speed, landscape, cities long drowned. But to Nerissa, the squid is about darkness and depth, and it wallows down here, holding them still.

Herman climbs up from the deck below, stretching at the top rung. "You need some tea," he says. "And, James, now you're allowed up here, don't take offence, but you need a shower."

"Use my quarters," says Nerissa, the ghost of a smile forming. "Up one flight over there."

"Okay, thanks. I really can't smell myself anymore."

Herman busies himself with mugs and water, clattering about at the sink.

"I've put Molloy in some fresh bedding for the night," he says over his shoulder. "Nice and secure. I'm glad to see him, but the little blighter seems sad. It's a shame he'll never have a mate. Such a thing is lonely as the sea itself."

Lights

Darshana Hardy is on the screen, her deep, almond-shaped eyes blinking. Her hair has fallen in strands from her tight bun. Rudolf is with them again. He holds two wires together from a damaged monitor; if he shifts, the image of the first officer fuzzes over and her voice turns low or disappears. Captain Holmes sits between Nerissa and Herman in Nerissa's reading chair.

"He's a criminal," says Hardy. "And you must return him to us. You aren't safe with him."

"He tells us we have been close to land, and that you want to keep us aboard."

Hardy's eyelids flicker. She looks away, at someone they cannot see.

"Not true. You have no idea what kind of dangers you have been saved from. How treasured you all are. You especially."

"What do you mean me?" asks Nerissa.

"You will be the first to give birth on board. Your baby will be the first generation on the ship. We will have a great ceremony for it."

Nerissa crosses her arm in front of her torso and steps back. If her baby is not one of them, this ceremony might be quite different. She imagines it for a flicker of a moment, and then banishes the thought.

"We treasure you." Darshana smiles, and all at once, every kindly steward, with their utility belt and their gentle voice, seems menacing.

"This doesn't matter," says Holmes. "What matters is only the truth. I know we have found land. I know it is possible to leave the ship."

Darshana keeps her eyes on Nerissa. "You trust him?" she says. "You take his word for it? Do you know what he has done? We are compassionate. We gave him a second chance. There is no land. He simply wanted to take control, to find his country again, to lead the *Baleen* on a wild goose chase. He's selfish. Hasn't it occurred to you that nothing changes?"

Holmes is speechless for a moment, then snorts.

"Why would I do that?" He looks from Herman to Rudolf to Nerissa. Rudolf is impassive, holding the two wires. Herman narrows his eyes.

"Anyway," says Holmes, "you've got nothing here. You don't know how to escape that creature. You know we won't last long down here. Let us speak to Esther."

"We're working on it. Esther is busy. She will not speak to you now."

"Oh, yes, so what have you come up with?"

"I-I would have to—It hardly matters. You must be in custody. You are mutinous."

"We'll run out of oxygen. You know that. What will you do? Kill a few less important people to give your treasured ones a couple more days? Perhaps the older ones, the scientists that put all this together? Or some younger ones, maybe, save initiating them. Perhaps the rebellious ones, ones showing signs of turning against you. Doesn't sound like utopia to me."

There is silence. Hardy rises from her seat, leaving them looking at an empty, sloping room.

"Just so you know," says Holmes to the empty seat, "we *do* have an idea. It really might work. We've bashed it out together. And we don't need much to try it. We don't need anything, in fact. Quite the opposite."

Nerissa sighs. Rudolf relaxes his hands, and the image flickers for a moment. When it returns, Esther Mortimer is sitting in Darshana's seat. She is wearing a blue velvet shirt buttoned tightly over her bust. Her lips shine. She arches an eyebrow.

"What is it you propose?"

"I'm almost certain," says Holmes, "that this idea will work. But we'll only try if you tell everyone aboard the truth and give them the choice to travel to dry land if they want to. Let them decide."

She lowers her eyes for a moment, then lifts her chin and stares back.

"You realise anything could be out there. If people go to land, they may die. We don't know if there are any survivors, or what their reaction will be. Here, everyone will be safe. Why risk that? More than that, why contaminate our strength with their weakness? Everyone here has agreed to be part of a new race. And someday … "

"Someday is not good enough," says Nerissa.

"And anyway," says Rudolf, "it isn't up to you. No one has agreed to stay underwater forever. Everyone thinks our aim is to find new land, to create a new life there."

"Let me back on the bridge," says Holmes, "and I'll try our plan. Do anything to me, and the plan is lost. We don't have long. Don't you already feel breathless?"

She looks away. Then she stands up, leaning down towards the screen, her teeth glimmering as she speaks.

"I won't agree to your terms. I will agree to only this: Nerissa may leave, then, if her child is not altered, it won't affect our project. It pains me, Nerissa," she says, coming even closer, her eyes enlarged and bright on the screen, "to lose you. But I can see now, you will never do as I ask. Rudolf, Herman, Leopold, if you want to go, then go. Holmes—go. I want no one here who does not support Mithras. No one else will know about the land."

She looks hard at Nerissa and then ends the transmission.

Nerissa dusts Holmes down with a horse-brush, slapping at the lapels of his jacket. She settles his peaked cap on his head.

"You'll do," she says.

"It'll take me ages to get up there: service lifts, ladders."

"I'll come," says Herman, "make sure you're okay. I've always wanted to go up there."

"All right. If it works, we'll see you two again in the daylight."

Herman squeezes Nerissa's shoulder, and she watches them both climb the ladder, Herman's heavy boots disappearing last.

Rudolf is in her reading chair, head in hands.

"What's up?" she says, perching next to him. "We did good, didn't we?"

"Yes," he says, taking her hand. "It's Dad. I didn't want to say. He's not well. After you met Holmes, after he heard his story, I took him back to repair some of the cities. He's heartbroken about all that work now damaged."

Rudolf pauses, takes a ragged breath. "We quarrelled too. He won't forgive me for not telling him about the captain, and about land. Because of Mum; he thinks she could still be alive. That she's out there somewhere. I doubt that. She's not, I'm almost certain. He believed in Mithras. He thought that they were doing something good. He feels betrayed. He took to his bed. It's like he's given up. He has some symptoms."

"Symptoms?"

"Of a stroke, or early dementia, I think. I can't be sure. It's as though all this has triggered something."

"Would you let me speak to him?"

"It might help."

"Let me get things ready down here, then." Nerissa begins switching off the lights, and Rudolf follows her. They descend to the animals and turn of the dim illumination until all they can sense is the sound of breathing, the snuffles and flickers, and the musty, rich smells. They switch on torches and get ready for the series of service lifts and slanting ladders that will take them to Leopold.

The glass cities look almost perfect from a few feet away, but as she comes close Nerissa sees the fissures in the buildings, the fallen domes and shattered windows, the cracked lakes and broken bridges. Rudolf takes her to his father's bed. Leopold is slumped into his pillow, eyes half-closed, his tanned, etched face slack, a brown woollen blanket tucked under his arms. He opens his eyes wider when he sees her.

"Young lady," he croaks, "what are you doing up at this time of night?"

"He's confused," whispers Rudolf.

"It's actually still early," Nerissa says brightly, holding up Greg's watch.

Leopold catches hold of her wrist. "That's a lovely time piece," he says, "but a bit big for you."

"It was my husband's."

"Of course. And where is he?"

"Dad," says Rudolf, and Leopold raises his eyebrows.

"I don't know," says Nerissa.

Leopold sighs and closes his eyes. He continues to speak.

"I had a dream," he says. "A giant squid was wrapped around our vessel and would not let go. Absurd. One gets ridiculous when one is old."

"It's actually real. It's not a dream."

He breathes in, opens one eye wide.

"Really? And what do you propose to do about it, then? You two think you are so clever."

"Dad."

"It's okay. We think the squid is lonely and looking for a mate."

"A case of mistaken identity?"

"Exactly. And we think part of our attraction is the light we emit."

"Your attraction? The light you emit? What gave you that idea?"

"Not *my* attraction. The ship. Us. The *Baleen*. It was Arthur C. Clarke, actually, that gave us that idea."

"Typical."

Nerissa looks at him, and then passes her hand over his brow. "So, we're just going to switch off our lights. Every last one. Outside and in. Every lamp. Every torch. Every LED. We'll stay pitch-dark and silent until it lets go. We'll rise back to the surface in the darkness."

"Pitch-dark," says Leopold, "like tar."

"Why don't you sleep now, Dad?" says Rudolf. "I'll check on you later."

"We wanted to do something great," he says, and turns away from them both to lie on his side.

Not long after, Holmes gives the order. Every light is turned off. The creatures outside disappear in the deep water, as if they were never there. Nerissa smiles at Rudolf, shining her torch up into her face, taking his hand. Then she switches it off. In the total darkness she hears Rudolf's nervous breathing and her own heartbeat. The baby stills, as if it knows. She could be in the sea, floating away, tethered to nothing.

Elsewhere in the ship, Gus holds Marie against his chest. Nick crouches in the kitchen, his hand against the cold oven door. Nick hates the dark. The Laundry women sit around their card table, knees touching. The schoolchildren huddle in the reading corner. And in the silence and the darkness, which seems to bend time so that no one knows how long, people remember what they have tried not to remember: the people left behind. The great uncle. The old university buddy. Every face blotted out for months. And everyone wonders what it would have been like to be ordinary, not changed, nothing special, and to stay and be with everyone else. Not to take only a husband or a child, but be with everyone and let the sea come over.

Greg

In the dark of the silent *Baleen,* no one can see the thick, salty tears roll down her cheeks. She thinks only of Greg, who did not come. Esther's story must be wrong in some way. It is not the Greg she knows. Perhaps Esther told him a lie, that Nerissa did not want him to join them. Now she's breathed a tiny breath into the idea that he's still alive, though she cannot imagine it is true. For two months she lived in that near-empty high-rise, believing him dead. She boarded the *Baleen,* believing him dead. Now that she knows he wasn't then, he must die all over again. Greg starving in a derelict house. Greg trudging into the hills barefoot, until his body drops and he dies staring at the cold stars. Or Greg in the sea. Greg most likely in the sea, diving, looking at something in wonder, when the great wave comes, dragging him along the seabed like debris. Greg drowned, washing up on a silent beach with so many other corpses, his lovely body bloated, arms and legs stuck out, his face blackened and unrecognisable. Even she would not know him.

She holds her breath. Something gives and creaks. There is a sucking, juddering sensation in the curved walls, the giant squid peeling away. Letting go. The ship gives a metallic groan. A jolt sends her into Rudolf's torso. He pushes back into her to steady them both. Slowly they rise and the ship rights itself, wobbling and tilting and heading up. She thinks of the squid, forlorn, realising the light and life has gone from its mate. She can only imagine it, huge and white and billowing away like a spectre.

Altereds

Leopold will go with them. His mind drifts in and out of strange states, but he says that he wants to come, and for hours at a time he is his usual self. Rudolf tells Nerissa Leopold's dementia is progressive, that he will need a lot of help, but sometimes he will be fine. After they surface, when he sees the daylight, Leopold is bright. He turns to Nerissa.

"Will you miss her?" he says.

"Who?" she asks, rubbing his shoulder.

"The squid."

She does not know what to say, imagining its white body deep below them, its huge, mournful eyes. She thinks of the clouds above the highway again, her father's gaze intent on the road.

"Maybe I'll dream about her," she says, and the answer seems to satisfy Leopold, who pats her hand and turns back to his packing.

"I will look at the cities," he says over his shoulder. "Just once more. But I must let them go."

Rudolf busies himself with preparations, helping Captain Holmes adapt the lifeboat that will take them away from the *Baleen*. Esther has kept her word, but they must tell no one else, and they must leave quickly, taking very little with them. They will be allowed onto the upper deck at night, to take few supplies, to leave all animals except Molloy. Nerissa thinks of the orangutan in the darkness of Esther's chamber.

Nerissa walks Deck Five, watching the vendors repairing the stalls and arranging their goods for the day. The sea beyond the portholes is calm and turquoise, the sky a shining silver. People are busying themselves with vegetables, tools, and clothes. These people who are not ordinary, who may become the only ones left.

"Ah, ma chère amie." Gus leans over the counter of the *Crêperie*, which crackles with the scent of vanilla and lemon.

"Just lemon," she says, smiling at him.

He turns down his mouth and shrugs. "You know, you should be happy. You seem glum. We are back nice and straight, like a train on a track. We are together."

"I know what you mean." She bites into the warm crêpe. She looks around her at everyone, working together to set things right. Trading their goods. Mending what they have. Talking to one another. She can hardly believe they are any different from ordinary people.

"You must come to our cabin," he says, scraping the hot plate clean. "We'd love you to come, for supper. Marie thinks you need to make more friends. So shy, she says, the shyest one I have met!"

Nerissa smiles. "I'd like to do that. Soon."

"Good. We can talk more. You can tell us about your life. About the things you will do next, here, in this new life. This better life."

Deck Twelve

Nerissa goes down to the animals for the last time. Night is coming; the natural dusky light filtering down tells her so. Rabbits twitch in their enclosures. She scoops one up and lifts it to her face, catching its back legs mid-run. The softest part of a rabbit is the strip of fur just at the back of its neck. It feels like silk. She presses her nose gently against it for the scent of washing drying outside in the air. That's the only way to describe the smell of rabbit fur. Perhaps she will smell that again out in the ruined, waterlogged fields. The clockwork mantis is still there, one friable limb poised as if time has stopped. And Reva the elephant, her heady musk, her dry prehistoric skin, her watery black eyes. She uncurls her trunk and flattens its wetness over Nerissa's chest, then down to her belly, as if she knows someone else is growing there, just like her own baby, pulsing and hot and close to seeing the world. Reva's baby will be born here, down in the dark, and who knows how it will fare. If it ever touches dry land, will the gravity be too much? Will the blue sky and hard soil hurt? Shem for a boy, Ruth for a girl. Nerissa scratches Reva between the eyes, the closest she can get to goodbye.

Lifeboat

In the early hours of the morning they climb out of the hatch and onto Deck One. There is a thin line of indigo to the east horizon. The heaped clouds look almost solid, like hills. The cool, fresh air feels like water after a long thirst; it lifts the hairs at the back of Nerissa's neck. Herman, Holmes, and Rudolf help Leopold, who breathes a deep breath above decks and will not look at Esther. Leopold turns to Rudolf and quietly says, "Is she out there, do you think? Waiting for us?"

Rudolf frowns for a moment, wondering whom he means, then says, "Quite possibly, Dad. Who knows what is out there." He helps Leopold down into the boat and spreads a blanket over his legs.

"Where are we going?"

Rudolf pauses, looking out to the lightening sky. "I'm not sure."

They load the lifeboat with their few supplies. Nerissa holds Molloy in a carry-cage. The only animal she is allowed to take. She feels him shifting restlessly inside. Esther looks on, wrapped in a cashmere scarf against the cold, her hair whipping away in the breeze, Darshana silent at her side. Esther is pale, her lips without their usual vermillion flash, her gloss diminished in the harsher light of a growing dawn.

"I'm sad to lose you, Nerissa," she says. "After everything. Are you sure you want to go out there?" She gestures to the empty horizon. "Who knows what state the world is in; what is left."

"I won't stay here," says Nerissa. "I will take my baby somewhere we will both be welcome."

Esther smiles thinly. "Your baby may well be one of us. And if not, well, you can try again with someone here. I don't think you will find any kind of welcome out there. You will get over your grief, which blinds you. You will forget Greg in time. He did the right thing. He was able to let go."

"Don't ever say his name again. Don't ever speak of him again as if he is already dead," says Nerissa with a fierceness that surprises her.

"He will be dead," says Darshana, suddenly, her reedy voice faint in the breeze, "by now." Esther touches Darshana's arm, and gives her a look, to hush her.

"He won't be the only one," she says. "And those who aren't, well, I cannot imagine ..."

"We'll take our chances," says Rudolf, appearing at Nerissa's side. He takes Molloy's cage from her grip. "Are we ready?"

Nerissa nods, following Rudolf and Holmes to the lifeboat, its canopy drawn down, its hull filled with supplies. The air tastes bright and salty.

"We've got good weather," says Holmes.

Herman wavers at the lifeboat's edge.

"Herman," says Nerissa, "where is all your stuff?"

Herman reaches out and takes her forearm, wrapping his gnarled hands around her thin muscle.

"I'm not coming this time," he says, looking her in the eye.

"Not coming, why?"

"This is where I want to be. There are the animals to care for. I said I could help on Garden Deck. I will work on the glass cities. I'm useful here."

"You'll be useful on land, Herm."

Nerissa grabs his hand as if to glue it to her arm.

"I can't face that life," he says, holding her gaze. "You know that. You'll be fine without me. You have your baby to think of."

Nerissa can't speak. He rubs a tear from her face with a rough thumb.

"Will you forgive me?" he says. "I'm not altered. I was only here for my knowledge of the science; it's not as if I could have told you what it was like to be … like you."

"There's nothing to forgive, Herman." She reaches up to his ear to whisper, "Do one thing for me. Look out for that lonely orangutan."

He nods and puts his russety arms around her and holds tight. She feels the wiry muscles in his back and grabs a clump of his shirt. Nerissa's forearms tingle for a moment, and she breathes in hard. She thinks of all the creatures she has cared for, whom she will never see again. She thinks of Reva the elephant, with her knowing, liquid eyes. Reva who will give birth in the submarine light to a baby that may never set its feet on land.

They board the lifeboat, joining Leopold, not knowing how far land might be. The horizon lightens.

"Ready?" says Captain Holmes.

"Ready," they say, and are released, the water splashing up as they fall into it. Molloy's camera captures the two women, and Herman, silhouetted on the deck of the *Baleen*. Esther's scarf flaps out beside her, like a crow's wing. And then they turn to go below. As the sun rises, red in the grey sky, the *Baleen* sinks back beneath the water.

Acknowledgements

I would like to thank the following people for supporting the writing of this novel:

Donald Winchester at *Watson, Little* for his belief in the book and unflagging help in developing it.

Cloud Lodge Books for their daring publishing ethos and beautiful books.

Miles Mitchard for love, support and grammatical skills.

The following people who have read and commented on early drafts: Luke Kennard, Liesl King, Naomi Booth, and Nicholas Royle.

Illustrator Alice Shirley and Natural History Museum curator Jon Ablett, for squid-related inspiration.

My family, for telling me for as long as I can remember that I could be a writer.

This book is dedicated to my son, Gabriel, who I hope will have the opportunity to meet woolly rats and orangutans in his lifetime.